QUEST FOR THE

Austral Amulet

Troy C Wilson

BiblioSky

ALSO BY TROY C. WILSON

Fiction
Love's Lifeline
(under pen name, Julian T. Westwood)
The Great Bugatti Heist
(with James Wilson)
Calm Cove

Non-Fiction
It's the Little Things: Transforming Your Marriage One Day at a Time
Love Beyond Conflict

Paperback ISBN: 978-0975612224

Published By BiblioSky Publishing – A Division of Skyward Media & Publications

Book Cover Idea and Design by Troy C Wilson

Illustrations by Book Brush

1st Edition 2024

www.bibliosky.com

Contents

For My Daughter, Rebecca
With All My Love, Dad

Chapter 1

I perched on the edge of the plush armchair, fingers tangled together to still their trembling. The lawyer's office cocooned us in a bubble removed from time, heavy with the scent of old books and the quiet tick of a grandfather clock. Here, in this moment, I felt the weight of the dividing line between my before and after. Glancing at the faces of my family, each lost in their own expectations and disappointments, I found solace in the muted ambiance, the lawyer's voice droning on in the background like a distant melody.

"To my nephew, Thomas," Mr. Penrose began, and just like that, the division of relics commenced. An ornate vase here, a set of fine china there—Great-Gran Eleanor's treasures distributed like cards in a high-stakes game.

Whispers coiled around each proclamation. Aunt Clara clasped her pearls as she was granted the grandfather clock; Uncle Martin's eyes gleamed at the mention of stocks and bonds. The artifacts of Eleanor's life reduced to commodities, pieces of her chiselled off and handed out.

Great Gran Eleanor's stories had always served as my sanctuary, my refuge from reality. With each recounting of my great-great grandfather, Jeremiah Harley's exploits, she crafted a world so rich and tangible that the ocean's salty mist seemed to lick my face, and the oppressive heat of the jungle appeared to envelop me. Those narratives extended beyond the realm of mere fables; they functioned as vital threads to a girl who frequently perceived herself as nothing more than a wraith in her own existence.

In those shared moments with Eleanor, our private world was real and tangible. She would chuckle softly, her eyes twinkling as she recounted her youth – stories laced with hidden wisdom that seemed meant just for me. Her words were like seeds planted deep within my mind, whispering promises of a life filled with purpose and adventure.

But outside of Eleanor's sunlit parlour, reality painted a different picture. At school, I moved through hallways like a spectre – present but unnoticed. Words would lodge in my throat as classmates chattered around me about things I couldn't quite grasp as important.

At home, it was much the same. My parents, wrapped up in their careers and social lives, often forgot to ask about my day or notice the books piled high on my desk – each one an escape hatch into another world where I wasn't so painfully invisible.

It was Eleanor who saw me – truly saw me – not just as her great-granddaughter but as Rebecca: a dreamer, a thinker, her emotions swirled like a tempest within, yet her lips remained sealed, as if words were fragile birds afraid to take flight from their cage." She'd often say with a knowing smile that one day I'd find my voice and when that day came, the world better watch out.

But confidence? That trait seemed to have skipped over me entirely. Whenever opportunity knocked, self-doubt answered first, chaining my feet to the ground while my heart yearned to soar.

Lost in thought, I nearly missed the rustle of paper as the solicitor adjusted his position and cleared his throat.

"...And to Rebecca Harley," he began, drawing my focus back to the present. The room hushed; even my parents leaned forward as if sensing an unexpected turn in this well-orchestrated ritual.

"I leave my personal diary," he continued, "in which I have documented many truths about our family history and some mysteries that I believe she alone has the heart to understand and resolve."

A collective gasp fluttered around the room like startled birds taking flight. Murmurs rose in volume as confused glances shot towards me. The diary? An actual written account from Eleanor? No one had known about its existence until this very moment.

My pulse quickened; every part of me buzzed with equal parts excitement and trepidation. This wasn't just any book; it was Great Gran's secret keeper, her confidant – now bequeathed to me as if she knew that I would need it most after she was gone.

Mr Penrose reached into his briefcase and pulled out an aged leather-bound journal that seemed to hum with silent stories. As he passed it to me, our fingertips met fleetingly, a silent exchange passing between us. In that brief touch, a weight seemed to shift, a solemn duty descending upon my shoulders like a cloak, unseen but palpable

I cradled it against my chest; its weight far heavier than its physical presence suggested. The room faded away as I traced my fingers over its worn cover; every scratch and crease whispered of secrets waiting just beneath its surface.

Eleanor had left me more than just pages filled with ink; she had left me a path – one that could lead me out of obscurity and into a life where I wasn't just background noise but someone with a story worth telling.

In that moment of realization, Great Gran's presence enveloped me once more; not through her voice or her touch but through this final gift that seemed to pulse with her belief in me.

As chatter swelled around me again about wills and legacies, none of it could pierce the bubble that Eleanor's diary created around us – it was just her and me once more in our own little world where anything seemed possible.

As I delicately lifted the leather-bound diary, its weight in my hands whispered of hidden wonders. Each touch seemed to unlock a fragment of the universe's enigma, as if cradling a precious whisper from the cosmos itself. It was much thicker than I had anticipated, edges worn, with whispers of countless pages pressed together like leaves preserved over time. The thought flickered across my mind – could this tome also hold the words of Jeremiah, my great-great-grandfather, the man whose blood thrummed with adventure in his veins?

As I held the diary close to my chest, a hushed resonance enveloped me, a gentle thrumming that seemed to emanate from its very pages. The cool touch of the leather against my palms whispered of stories untold, inviting me into a world of secrets and revelations. With each heartbeat, the diary became more than just an object; it became a conduit to the past, a tangible link to the mysteries waiting to be unveiled. The pendant around my neck, a tangible memory of Eleanor, seemed to pulse with warmth as if it recognized the significance of the moment. The possibility that I held not just one diary but several stitched together under one cover was a tantalizing thought. Maybe Eleanor and Jeremiah's spirits were entwined within these pages.

Around me, the murmur of relatives echoed like a distant storm, their curious eyes glinting with unspoken questions. I caught snippets of their conversation, hungry for any morsel that might reveal more about Eleanor's life or, perhaps more greedily, anything that would elevate their own status through association.

"Becca, don't you want to see what's inside?" Aunt Margery's voice slithered over to me. Her eyes bore into me like drills.

I shifted uncomfortably but managed a small smile. "I think I'll wait for a bit. It feels right to have some privacy when I read it."

Uncle Harold leaned in, his breath reeking of coffee and insincerity. "But surely there are things about the family we all ought to know?"

My grip on the diary tightened defensively. "Eleanor trusted me with this," I said determinedly. "It's not just about family secrets; it's her trust."

They exchanged glances, unsatisfied but unable to argue against the dead's last wishes. With nods and shrugs, they dispersed back into their cliques, no doubt concocting new strategies to pry open Eleanor's world.

As soon as decency allowed, I excused myself from the suffocating room filled with voracious eyes and whispers that clung like cobwebs. My heart pounded a frantic rhythm as I made my way home.

⸺ • ◦ ◉ ◦ • ⸺

Within the walls of our house, familiarity seemed elusive, as if each room were but a temporary stop for passing travelers. Conversations echoed hollowly, and the air held a sense of detachment, as though we were lodgers sharing a transient shelter rather than a family bound by shared history and belonging. Today it was blissfully empty – my parents and siblings back at the will reading – allowing me to slip unnoticed into the house.

The attic had always been my refuge; a place where dust motes danced like fairies in shafts of light and where silence was a comfortable blanket wrapped around me. The old wooden stairs creaked beneath my feet as I ascended into my sanctuary.

With trembling hands and bated breath, I positioned myself on an aged armchair whose fabric had seen better days. The key – small and ornate – dangled from its chain around my neck next to Eleanor's pendant. The lock on the diary was an old-fashioned one, seemingly forged from another era entirely.

The first attempt to insert the key met with resistance; age had not been kind to either lock or key. My fingers fumbled awkwardly around the mechanism as frustration crept up on me like ivy on an old wall.

7

"Come on," I whispered as if coaxing a shy animal out of hiding.

The second try was no better; the key refused to turn, stubborn as winter soil against a shovel. My heart sank with each failed attempt – would Eleanor's words remain sealed away from me?

On the third attempt, something shifted – not just within the lock but within me too. It was as if Eleanor herself guided my hand with gentle firmness born from years of patience and understanding. The key turned with an almost imperceptible click that resonated through every fiber of my being.

Slowly, ever so slowly, I opened the cover...

Opening the diary was like prying open a gateway to another world, a crypt that cradled whispers of the past. The leather cover, weathered by time, creaked as I coaxed it apart. My fingers traced the edges of several sections that had been delicately inserted into its pages.

I took a breath, the musty scent of aged paper flooding my senses. As I sat with the task at hand, a subtle but undeniable presence seemed to linger over my shoulder, a silent guardian from generations past. In the air, I could almost feel the weight of Great Gran's gaze, a blend of reassurance and the unspoken anticipation of upholding the family legacy. I imagined her hands, worn and gentle, once turning these same pages, weaving tales that had fuelled my dreams.

The first section held stories penned in Eleanor's elegant script. Her words danced across the page, recounting adventures of resilience and hope. I saw her not just as my great grandmother but as a young woman with fire in her eyes and an unquenchable thirst for life.

Tucked between the tales were photographs that told their own silent stories. There was Great Gran in her youth, standing beside a man whose eyes mirrored mine—Jeremiah Harley. Another showed her holding a child, her smile radiant and familiar. As my thumb traced the contours of the images, a profound sense of connection welled up within me, transcending the boundaries of time and space. Though they were strangers in the flesh, their faces captured in faded photographs stirred something deep within my soul. With each gentle stroke, I felt the echo of their existence—a silent acknowledgment of the lineage that bound us together across generations. It was as if their presence whispered through time, weaving a tapestry of shared experience and untold stories that resonated within me, connecting me to a past I had never known yet somehow felt intimately familiar with.

Letters from distant relatives nestled among the photos, their voices reaching out across generations with news of births, marriages, and the passing of loved ones. They spoke of a family tapestry rich with history and bound by shared blood.

And then there was an envelope. It was thick and bulged at the centre. On its front in Eleanor's hand read "For the Trip." My heart skipped. Inside was money—old bills that seemed untouched by time—evidence of a journey intended but never embarked upon.

With reverence, I placed the envelope aside and delved deeper into the diary's secrets. It wasn't until I reached a tattered old leather-bound document that my breath caught in my throat. The heading emblazoned across it read "The Search for the Austral Amulet."

This was it—the heart of Jeremiah's legacy. I unfolded the document with trembling hands, revealing pages upon pages of meticulous instructions, maps crisscrossed with routes, and diagrams that whispered of hidden mechanisms.

Jeremiah's writing was firm and decisive, each word etched with purpose. He spoke of challenges faced and knowledge gained on his quest for the Austral Amulet—his life's work laid bare on these brittle pages.

The maps were a cartographer's dream: detailed sketches of landscapes both lush and barren, dotted with symbols that beckoned to secrets just beyond reach. Each route seemed to tell a story of trials overcome and wisdom earned.

As I turned each page, absorbing every word, I pieced together the essence of Jeremiah Harley—a man who had poured his soul into this search with unwavering conviction.

I could almost hear his voice guiding me through his notes:

"Mind the setting sun as it kisses the edge of Mount Gilead; there lies your first clue," he wrote beneath a sketch of rugged peaks bathed in golden light.

And further on: "Trust not only your eyes but also your spirit; it will lead where maps cannot."

The diagrams puzzled me at first—complex sequences of locks and keys, hidden compartments within ancient statues, and cryptic symbols whose meanings were lost to time. But as I studied them closer, intuition began to dance within me—a language beyond words whispering its secrets.

My eyes grew wide when I uncovered Jeremiah's final entry—a solemn vow etched onto a page worn thin:

"I leave this legacy not as an unfinished chapter but as an invitation for those who dare to dream as I did."

His words echoed in my heart: an invitation—and perhaps a challenge—to step beyond the ordinary into a world brimming with adventure.

I realized then that this document wasn't merely a record; it was part of me now—a piece of my heritage calling out across time for completion.

Clutching Jeremiah's legacy to my chest, I sat back against the musty walls of my attic sanctuary. The world outside faded away as possibility after possibility played out in my mind's eye.

Would I follow this path laid out by ancestors whose blood coursed through my veins.

I brushed a stray lock of hair from my face, the pendant around my neck catching the dim light in the attic as I flipped through the pages of this old document.

My fingers traced the faded ink, absorbing each word like a sponge. Why was this amulet so important to Jeremiah Harley? My eyes flickered to his portrait etched on the page—a stern look on his face, as if he were challenging me to understand his obsession. He never found it; the journey had claimed him before he could even start. I imagined him, his spirit restless, wandering in search of peace that could only come from completing his quest.

The Austral Amulet... what secrets did you hold?

The next section of Jeremiah's writings unveiled more than just an adventure—it spoke of a curse, one that wound through our family tree like ivy, choking its growth with misfortune and sorrow. My hands trembled as I read about our lineage's burden, one that stretched back centuries. A curse that no one ever spoke of but seemed to linger in hushed tones at family gatherings and in the shadows of our home.

Jeremiah believed in the Amulet's power to break this curse. It was more than just a treasure hunt; it was redemption for our bloodline. The realization hit me like a cold splash—this wasn't just his story; it was mine too.

I closed my eyes for a moment, allowing myself to absorb the weight of what lay before me. This wasn't just an inheritance; it was a call to action. A mission passed down through generations until it landed in my hands—the least likely of heroes.

But could I? A thirteen-year-old girl with nothing but a penchant for daydreams and solitude?

Downstairs, my relatives' voices were a distant buzz, none wiser to the secret legacy nestled between these leather-bound covers. They would laugh at the idea—dismiss it as fantasy or forbid me from even considering such folly.

No. This was between Eleanor and me.

She knew me—the real Rebecca Harley—a dreamer with a thirst for something more than this small-town existence could quench. She understood my longing for adventure because it mirrored her own and perhaps Jeremiah's too. She left me this diary not just as a keepsake but as a beacon—a guiding light towards my destiny.

A surge of determination swelled within me. This journey was dangerous, undoubtedly filled with challenges that would test every ounce of courage I didn't know I possessed. Yet, wasn't this what I'd always yearned for? An escape from invisibility? A chance to prove myself—to them and to me?

I glanced at the envelope marked "For the Trip." Eleanor had planned for this moment; she believed in me before I ever dared to believe in myself.

I could hear her voice now, gentle yet firm, "Rebecca, be who you are meant to be."

The words wrapped around me like armor. The attic, once a sanctuary of solace, now beckoned as a threshold of beginnings. Here, amidst the shadows of forgotten relics, Rebecca Harley sensed the stirring of her own narrative, where her identity would transcend the mere whispers of history, and she would emerge from the cloak of anonymity to claim her rightful place among the cherished heirlooms.

I tucked Jeremiah's document safely back into its place within the diary and slipped it under my arm. The pendant at my neck seemed to pulse with new life—as if Eleanor's spirit were there with me, urging me forward.

Quietly descending from my refuge, I returned to the world below where the family had returned and life carried on as usual—unaware that everything was about to change.

With each deliberate stride toward my room, anticipation swelled within me like a rising tide. The tasks of packing and planning became more than mere chores; they were affirmations of purpose. Each item carefully chosen, each plan meticulously laid out, fortified my resolve, casting aside doubt and ushering in a profound sense of assurance. This journey would reveal not only the secret power of the Austral Amulet but also unlock who Rebecca Harley truly was—who she was meant to be—and where she fit into this vast tapestry we call life.

It wasn't just about breaking curses or finding amulets; it was about finding myself in the process.

Hence, I decided to set out at daybreak, prior to the awakening of the household. Brimming with a fresh sense of resolve, I began to craft my own narrative in the epic—a legacy passed down to me from Great Gran Eleanor, one that I was destined to accomplish.

This voyage would not merely mimic Jeremiah's incomplete odyssey; it would be a trail I blazed with bravery I had not realised slumbered inside me.

"Rebecca? You awake?" My mother's voice seeped through the wood, soft yet insistent.

I scrambled to hide the diary under my pillow before calling out, "Yeah! Just reading."

Her silhouette paused at my door before retreating—another night where words remained unspoken between us.

Alone once more, I drew out the diary and gazed at it anew. My journey had begun without a single step taken outside my room. It was written in these pages—the call to adventure that resonated with something deep within me—and it promised to lead me towards not only finding myself but perhaps mending a fractured lineage with unity and understanding.

"Am I really brave enough?" The question escaped my lips in a whisper, dissolving into the stillness of my room. It wasn't just about bravery; it was about belonging. This quest could be my chance to carve out a place where I fit perfectly—where no one would overlook me or dismiss me as just another face in the crowd.

My ancestors' blood ran through my veins; their spirit seemed to whisper encouragement from within these aged pages. Yet there was something daunting about stepping into their world—a world where every choice carried weight and consequences stretched far beyond what I could foresee.

As sleep beckoned with gentle insistence, I placed the diary on my nightstand—the lock now undone but its contents still brimming with secrets yet to be revealed. Tonight had been an awakening; tomorrow would be the first step on a path laid out by destiny's hand.

The map would wait until morning; for now, dreams would carry me along rivers of starlight and into lands where echoes of Jeremiah's footsteps still lingered in wait for mine to join them in their timeless dance.

Chapter 2

The first rays of sunlight had barely touched the horizon when I slipped out of my bedroom window, the diary secured in my backpack along with a few hastily packed essentials. The weight of the book against my back was comforting, like a steady hand guiding me forward. My heart thrummed with a cocktail of nerves and excitement; this was the moment my life took a sharp turn toward the unknown.

I'd never ventured far from Wollow Creek on my own, but the thrill of responsibility and adventure that Eleanor had always spoken of pulsed through me. As I embarked on my journey, the pendant nestled against my skin seemed to radiate warmth, as if offering its silent blessing to my chosen path. With each stride away from the familiarity of home, I sensed a subtle shift within myself. Like shedding layers of an old skin, I felt the weight of doubt and hesitation begin to dissipate, replaced by a burgeoning courage that had long lain dormant within. The journey ahead promised not just adventure, but a journey of self-discovery, where the old, timid Rebecca would gradually give way to a newer, bolder version of herself.

My thoughts drifted to Isaac as I made my way through the quiet streets. We had been thick as thieves as kids, imagining ourselves as explorers in uncharted territories right here in our own backyards. But time had wedged distance between us, and our last encounter had left a frosty silence in its wake. Still, if anyone in Wollow Creek craved adventure as much as I did, it was Isaac.

His house loomed ahead, modest, and familiar. I hesitated at the gate, chewing on my lip. Could I bridge the gap that had formed between us? Did he still see me as that timid girl he used to protect? Gathering every shred of newfound courage, I pushed open the gate and walked up to his door.

The knock seemed to echo louder than I intended in the stillness of dawn. Moments later, Isaac's face appeared at the doorway, sleep-ruffled hair and eyes blinking away confusion.

"Rebecca? What're you doing here so early?"

"I need your help," I blurted out before doubt could silence me.

His brows knitted together as he stepped outside, closing the door behind him to keep from waking his family. "What kind of help?"

I shifted from one foot to another, clutching my backpack straps. "It's... it's about an amulet. And a curse."

He studied me for a long moment before nodding for me to continue.

I explained everything – Eleanor's stories, her will reading gift, Jeremiah's diary with its maps and cryptic instructions about the Austral Amulet. Isaac listened without interrupting, his expression unreadable.

When I finished, an unsettling silence stretched between us.

"You're serious about this?" His voice was steady but his eyes betrayed concern.

"I've never been more serious about anything."

He ran a hand through his hair and sighed. "Rebecca, this isn't some childhood game. It's dangerous."

"I know," I said. "That's why I came to you."

Isaac leaned against the porch railing, considering. "And what if your family finds out you're gone?"

"I left a note," I lied smoothly. The truth was that they wouldn't notice until well into the day; by then I intended to be too far to easily retrieve.

He eyed me with newfound respect mingled with worry. "You've really thought this through."

"It's something I have to do." My voice was firm despite the tremor inside.

As a car rumbled past on the quiet street behind us, its presence a rare disturbance in our typically tranquil town, Isaac's gaze followed its path until it vanished around the corner. With a thoughtful expression, he eventually turned his attention back to me, a silent question lingering in his eyes.

"And you want me to come with you?"

I nodded earnestly. "You're the only one who understands what it's like to want more than what Wollow Creek has to offer."

Isaac pushed off from the railing and paced a few steps before stopping and facing me again. The sky was brighter now; morning had officially broken.

"Okay," he finally said with a resolute nod. "I'll come."

Relief washed over me like a warm wave.

"But," he continued with an authoritative finger pointed at me, "we do this right. No rushing into things without planning."

"Of course," I agreed.

He gave a half-smile then – that familiar grin that used to mean we were about to embark on some mischievous plan concocted under willow trees and summer skies.

"We'll need supplies," he started listing immediately. "Food, water, gear..."

My smile matched his as we fell into an easy rhythm discussing logistics; for those moments it was like nothing had ever changed between us.

Isaac's eyes moved from his dwelling to mine, resolve carved into his expression. "An hour," he declared. "Let's reconvene here afterward."

"You swear you won't share this with anyone?" I asked, my voice laced with apprehension.

His smile, a beacon of assurance, washed away any lingering doubts. 'Our secret escapade? My lips are sealed. My parents won't even know you stopped by,' he whispered, sealing the pact with a conspiratorial wink.

With that promise enveloping us like a cloak, we crossed the threshold into his home. In each step, a buoyancy lifted me, a sensation foreign yet exhilarating. It was as though the weight of uncertainty had been replaced by the airy wings of anticipation, propelling me forward into the unknown with a newfound sense of freedom.

With Isaac Thorne now by my side, his familiar presence transformed from protector to fellow adventurer, the boundaries of Wollow Creek seemed to shrink into insignificance. What was once our safe haven now resembled nothing more than a fading starting line, disappearing into the distance behind us as we set forth into the vast expanse of the unknown. With each stride forward, the world expanded before us, beckoning us toward new horizons and boundless possibilities.

An hour later, Isaac and I tossed our backpacks into the rear of his well-worn Jeep. The motor sputtered awake, more hesitant than either of us to embark on this adventure. I gripped Eleanor's journal tightly, its leather binding offering a comforting chill to my hand.

Isaac maneuvered through the streets with a confidence I envied. The hum of the engine and the rhythmic swipe of wipers against a misting rain were our only soundtrack. We had supplies to gather, yet neither of us knew where to start. It was like trying to piece together a puzzle without knowing what the picture was.

Isaac looped around Wollow Creek's centre twice before his hand struck the steering wheel. "Hold on, something from the town newspaper comes to mind—someone who could assist us," he declared, his brow furrowing as he delved into his recollections like shuffling through a deck of cards.

"It was about a Doctor—her name eludes me. She's a historian from around here, renowned for her skill in deciphering old enigmas."

His enthusiasm spread to me, yet it swiftly became apparent we had no idea where to locate this historian. We ended up at Isaac's workshop, a place redolent with the scent of oil and neglected items. Rifling through a stack of newspapers, we scoured each edition in search of the story. Our digits skimmed line after line until halting on a feature about the historian—her name, Dr. Victoria Bellamy.

With new purpose, we set off to the next town where she worked at the local museum. Anticipation churned in my stomach with each mile we covered.

Our arrival in town coincided with a sinking realization—the museum stood silent, its doors locked tight behind yellow tape that read 'Renovations'. My heart sank as Isaac tried the handle anyway.

"No luck," he said, shaking his head.

We spent hours canvassing the town for Dr. Bellamy's whereabouts—each inquiry met with shrugs or vague gestures in various directions that led nowhere. Frustration bubbled up in me, an unwelcome companion to the cold that had settled in my bones.

Defeated by dusk, we retreated to Wollow Creek Library in search of anything about the Austral Amulet or hints on where to start our search. The library was quiet save for the tick of a clock reminding us that time was slipping away.

I skimmed through dusty volumes on mythology and ancient curses while Isaac scoured atlases and historical texts. But all we found were dead ends and closing time creeping up on us.

A sudden clatter echoed from a nearby aisle as books toppled from a high shelf. Isaac darted over just as a woman on a ladder teetered dangerously, her arms full of heavy tomes.

"Allow me to lend a hand," Isaac offered, stabilizing both the ladder and the woman with a firm grip.

I trailed him, craning my neck to glimpse our inadvertent rescuer—her dark locks secured haphazardly, spectacles teetering on the brink of her nose as she steadied herself against the shelving.

As Isaac aided her descent, he scrutinized her countenance briefly until realization dawned in his eyes.

"Dr. Bellamy!" he burst out, his voice echoing across the silent library corridors. "I've seen your photograph in the newspaper."

She looked up at him, startled, her eyes widening behind the lenses of her glasses. With a slight tilt of her head, she pushed her glasses up her nose, her brow arching inquisitively. "Yes? And who might you be?"

Encouraged by her curiosity, I stepped forward, a surge of newfound bravery coursing through me. "We've been searching for you all day," I started tentatively, feeling the weight of the moment. "You see, we're searching for this ancient amulet..."

"And, well, I believe you're the only one who can help us," I added earnestly, meeting her gaze with determination, silently pleading for her assistance.

She peered over her glasses, a curious gleam in her eyes. "What sort of help?"

With a steadying breath, I laid the diary on a nearby table and flipped it open to reveal Jeremiah's meticulous notes and the frayed edges of an ancient map. "It's about this," I said, pointing to the document that spoke of the Austral

Amulet. "My great-great-grandfather was searching for it, and I believe it's real."

Her eyes scanned the pages with a historian's precision. "Fascinating," she murmured. "And you wish to find this amulet?"

I nodded. "It's more than just a treasure hunt. It's about breaking a family curse and... and finding out who I am supposed to be."

Dr. Bellamy's fingers traced the lines of ink as if she could absorb their secrets through her skin. She lifted her gaze to meet mine, an unreadable expression etched on her face.

"You have quite the adventure ahead of you," she said.

Isaac leaned in closer, his blue eyes bright with anticipation. "We were hoping you might shed some light on this map and maybe some information on ancient artifacts like the amulet."

A smile cracked her professional demeanor for just a moment as she leaned back in her chair, folding her arms across her chest. "Well," she began, adjusting her glasses, "the markings here suggest a route used by traders centuries ago." Her finger danced along the faded lines and symbols that crisscrossed the paper.

Isaac and I exchanged glances—his eyes wide with wonder mirrored my own—as Dr. Bellamy continued to unravel the secrets of Jeremiah's notes.

"The script here is archaic, not commonly seen," she explained, pointing to an indecipherable scrawl at the corner of the map. "But it indicates a meeting place of sorts—a confluence of cultures where items like your amulet might have been traded or... hidden."

Her words wove a spell around us, and we hung on every syllable as if they were keys unlocking doors to hidden worlds.

"Dr. Bellamy," Isaac interjected, his voice breaking through my trance. "Would you consider joining us? We could really use someone with your expertise."

The question lingered in the air like smoke from an extinguished candlewick.

She hesitated, biting her lip in contemplation while drumming her fingers on the wooden table surface.

"My obligations here, my studies," she faltered, then gave us a determined look. "I need to mull it over... to confirm its authenticity rather than dismissing it as a long-lost tale from a bygone kin."

Examining Jeremiah's journal, "This journal is indeed captivating. Its contents align with historical records, and I'm familiar with the legend of a vanished amulet. "Could this be it... discovering such an artifact is the quintessence of a historian's aspirations. "If I decline, I'd be left with eternal curiosity."

"Yet..." She faltered once more, seemingly grappling with her own thoughts before resuming with an intensified conviction. "Yet how often is one presented with the opportunity to transition from the realm of these tomes to the theater of history itself?"

A subtle excitement surged within me upon hearing her declaration—a flicker of enthusiasm that appeared to awaken something in Dr. Bellamy too.

"Alright," she declared, her gradual nod appearing to intertwine our destinies. "I'm with you, but first, I must organize a couple of matters before our departure."

Isaac erupted in joy, while I permitted a modest grin—the first sincere one since this unexpected odyssey began.

"We should plan our route carefully," Dr. Bellamy suggested as we gathered around Jeremiah's map once more.

She spoke of travel visas and local guides, archaeological protocols, and potential dangers that lay in lands where lawlessness prevailed over order.

"The first piece appears to be located here," she said, tapping a finger on a coastal region marked by tiny inscriptions that none but Jeremiah had likely laid eyes upon for over a century.

"How do we even start looking for something so old?" Isaac asked, skepticism lining his brow.

Dr. Bellamy pushed up her glasses with an air of confidence that seemed to fill the room with light. "You start by understanding what you're looking for—the history behind it—the legends that give it life."

We listened intently as she outlined strategies for researching each potential location before setting foot there—a blend of historical context and modern practicality that would form our guideposts along this perilous path.

As night began to fall outside the library windows, casting long shadows across our makeshift meeting table, we delved deeper into logistics: supplies we would need, funds for unexpected expenses, contacts Dr. Bellamy had across various academic fields that could aid our quest.

Isaac's pen danced feverishly across the page, capturing every word uttered by Dr. Bellamy with frantic urgency. Meanwhile, I strained to absorb every syllable, my mind racing to imprint each detail into memory. Each word felt like a lifeline, each pause a potential pitfall. The weight of the information hung heavy in the air, each sentence a thread in the intricate tapestry of our quest. Missing even a single word threatened to unravel the delicate balance we sought, urging me to cling to each syllable as if it were a precious gemstone leading us closer to our goal.

She brought more than just knowledge; she brought legitimacy—a sense that what we were doing wasn't just some child's fantasy but a real expedition with tangible goals and profound implications.

We stood there—three disparate souls united by an ancient mystery—as plans solidified into actions steps and fears transformed into resolve.

This was no longer just my journey or Isaac's adventure; it was our quest—a shared odyssey charted across time-worn maps and bound by fate's unyielding hand.

Chapter 3

In the Harley household, morning light spilled across empty sheets where Rebecca should have been dreaming. The silence in her room hummed with the absence of her presence. Downstairs, the aroma of coffee did little to mask the growing concern etched on Jenny's face as she discovered her daughter's room vacant, bed untouched from the night before.

"Ted!" she called out, her voice cracking with urgency as she searched the quiet corners of their home. Ted appeared, his expression shifting from sleepy confusion to sharp alarm as he registered his wife's panic.

"Rebecca's not in her room," Jenny said, each word quivering like leaves in a storm.

Ted, his heart pounding against his chest, scoured the house, hoping for a sign of their daughter. His search ended in nothing but echoes of their own movements. "Did she say anything to you last night?" he asked, turning to Jenny with furrowed brows.

Jenny shook her head, her mind racing through the previous day's events. "She was so quiet at dinner... I thought she was just tired."

Frustration and fear mingled on Ted's face as he snatched up his phone to call neighbors and friends. Meanwhile, Jenny slumped into a chair at the kitchen table, her thoughts tumbling back through the years.

She remembered Rebecca as a child, bright-eyed and clinging to every word Eleanor spoke of far-off lands and ancient secrets. They had shared a bond unlike any other in the family; an unspoken understanding that flourished in their shared love for tales of adventure. Since Eleanor's passing, Rebecca had become more withdrawn than ever, as if a piece of her had faded with the old woman's last breath.

The grief that followed Eleanor's death seemed to hang over Rebecca like a shadow. Jenny recalled how her daughter would spend hours in the attic, poring over books and maps that once belonged to Great Gran. It was as if she was searching for something that could bridge the gap between them now that Eleanor was gone.

As Ted spoke with friends on the phone, Jenny's mind drifted back to a particular story Eleanor once told during one of their summer visits – a tale about Jeremiah Harley and his lifelong quest for an ancient artifact. It was a story filled with mystery and danger; one that always left Rebecca wide-eyed and hungry for more.

Could it be? Could Rebecca have taken those stories to heart? Was it possible that Eleanor's tales had inspired her granddaughter to embark on an adventure of her own?

The thought struck Jenny like a thunderclap. Her heart raced as she considered the possibility that Rebecca might be out there somewhere trying to follow in Jeremiah's footsteps.

"Ted," she whispered. "Eleanor used to tell stories... about your ancestor Jeremiah and some kind of quest he was on."

Ted paused mid-dial, his expression turning from one of action to contemplation. "You think this has something to do with Bec running off?"

"I don't know," Jenny admitted with a shrug of helplessness. "But those stories... they were special to her."

Ted set his phone down slowly as realization dawned on him too. The two parents sat in silence for a moment before he stood up decisively.

"We need to find out where she might have gone," he said with newfound resolve.

As Jenny nodded in agreement, a knot tightened in her stomach, a tumultuous blend of emotions swirling within her. Fear gripped her, tendrils of apprehension winding their way through her thoughts, as she contemplated the dangers that Rebecca might encounter on her journey. Guilt gnawed at her conscience, a heavy burden weighing down her heart, as she reflected on her failure to perceive the warning signs earlier. Each nod was a silent admission of her concerns, a silent plea for Rebecca's safety, mingled with the bitter sting of remorse for her own shortcomings.

As they began their search through Rebecca's room for clues—maps scattered across her desk, books about ancient civilizations stacked on shelves—it became clear that Eleanor's stories had left more than just memories behind; they had ignited a spark within Rebecca that had grown into a flame too fierce to be contained within these walls.

Amidst all this was the missing journal—Eleanor's last gift—and it seemed increasingly likely it held answers to questions they hadn't even thought to ask.

The truth hung heavy in the air: Rebecca had embarked on an adventure much like those spun by Great Gran's vivid imagination—a journey fueled by longing and loss, driven by curiosity and courage.

As Ted and Jenny combed through the remnants of their daughter's covert preparations, a profound sense of revelation washed over them. Each uncovered item unveiled a layer of Rebecca's hidden world, illuminating facets of her character that had remained veiled to them. Yet, amidst the discoveries, lingered a poignant awareness that they were merely scratching the surface of who Rebecca truly was and the path she was destined to tread. With each revelation, their understanding deepened, and the realization dawned that they were on the precipice of witnessing their daughter's transformation into the person she was meant to be.

As dusk settled and their worry deepened, Ted made yet another call—now to the local law enforcement—to declare Rebecca's disappearance, but their promises to exhaust all efforts in finding her brought him scant solace.

Jenny remained seated at the kitchen table, engrossed in contemplation, gripping a pendant with shaking hands—a mute entreaty for her daughter's well-being, wherever she might find herself beneath the expansive nocturnal heavens.

After concluding his conversation with the authorities, Ted approached Jenny at the table; his hand extended to envelop hers—a tacit pledge shared silently between them, confirming their resolve to recover their daughter regardless of the cost.

And so two quests unfolded beneath moonlit heavens—one driven by youthful courage seeking truth within family legend; another fueled by parental love desperate to bring their child home safely from whatever lay ahead on roads less traveled by those who came before them all in search of something lost yet forever sought after: The Astral Amulet—and answers lying hidden within its ancient gleam.

The evening sun dipped low as we sat in Dr. Bellamy's cozy study, surrounded by walls lined with books that seemed to whisper secrets of a thousand forgotten tales. Maps and charts lay scattered across the large oak desk, illuminated by the warm glow of a brass desk lamp. Dr. Bellamy had just returned from another room, arms laden with supplies: aged leather-bound journals, magnifying glasses, and a small digital recorder.

"I've always believed that the best way to prepare for any expedition is to anticipate every possible scenario," Dr. Bellamy explained, setting down the items with care.

Isaac rummaged through his backpack, pulling out the list we'd made at the library. "We've got most of the basics covered—food, water, first aid kit. But what about climbing gear? Or protection from... well, whatever we might find out there?"

I observed Dr. Bellamy nodding thoughtfully, her expression reflecting a calculated consideration of our needs. "Ropes and harnesses are essential," she affirmed, pen poised over her notepad as she made a quick note. "And when it comes to protection," she continued, peering at us over the rim of her glasses, "our greatest assets will be our intellect and resourcefulness."

Isaac chuckled. "Guess I should've paid more attention in those Boy Scout meetings."

Dr. Bellamy smiled and continued to list out additional supplies: torches, batteries, a satellite phone for emergencies.

My stomach twisted into knots as I contemplated the enormity of the journey ahead. Each item on our checklist served as a stark reminder of the daunting perils lurking on the horizon. The weight of responsibility pressed heavily upon my shoulders, each task a tangible manifestation of the obstacles we were bound to encounter. With each glance at the list, a shiver of apprehension coursed through me, underscoring the gravity of our undertaking and the uncertainties that awaited us at every turn.

Once our planning session came to a close and Isaac left to secure some final items from his garage, I excused myself for some fresh air. I wandered aimlessly through the quiet streets until I found myself standing at the edge of a park that overlooked my neighborhood.

From this distance, my house was just another silhouette against the twilight sky—its windows dark and lifeless. It looked so small, so inconsequential.

Wrapping my arms around myself, I felt a shiver run down my spine as a chill settled in the air. Eleanor's diary weighed heavily in my backpack, like a tangible piece of her essence tethered to me—a comforting presence that whispered words of encouragement whenever doubt threatened to overshadow my thoughts.

How many nights had I sat in my room, beneath the soft glow of my lamp, longing for adventure? And now here I was on the precipice of an actual quest—my quest—and fear gnawed at my insides.

I could almost hear Eleanor's voice in my head: "Adventure isn't about certainty, Rebecca; it's about discovering who you are when you step beyond what's known."

A tear escaped down my cheek as I gazed at my silent home one last time before turning away.

⸺ • ◉ • ⸺

The next morning arrived with an air of finality—the beginning of our true journey. Dr. Bellamy's place was abuzz with activity as we loaded up her rugged SUV with all our gear. Her meticulous attention to detail had not only ensured that everything on our list was secured but had gone above and beyond, leaving me feeling a deep sense of gratitude and newfound stability.

Isaac hoisted a backpack into the back and caught my eye with a knowing look—a mix of excitement and solemnity.

"We're really doing this," he said.

"Yeah," I replied, the gravity of his words sinking into my chest like a heavy stone.

Dr. Bellamy locked her front door and turned to us with an assertive nod. "This is it then."

She held out her hand—a gesture calling for unity—and Isaac placed his hand atop hers without hesitation.

I hesitated for just a moment before adding mine to the pile—a symbol of our shared commitment.

37

"Whatever happens out there," Dr. Bellamy said, "we face it together."

"Together," Isaac echoed.

And then it was my turn—the smallest voice in our trio but one that carried the weight of generations searching for answers hidden within an ancient amulet.

"Together," I affirmed, surprised by the strength that pulsed through that single word.

With one last glance at each other, we piled into the vehicle and set off into the breaking dawn—three souls bound by history and hope on a path paved with mysteries untold.

Chapter 4

In the sleepy town of Wollow Creek, the morning sun cast long shadows on the ground as the local police force began their search for Rebecca Harley and Isaac Thorne. The townspeople whispered in hushed tones, glancing at the fluttering papers taped to lampposts and storefront windows, each bearing the images of the missing youths. Officers canvassed the area, knocking on doors and interviewing anyone who might have caught a glimpse of Rebecca or Isaac.

At the local diner, a waitress with an eagle eye for detail recounted her encounter with the pair. "They were in a hurry," she said, pouring coffee for an officer taking notes.

"The girl seemed excited, like she was on some grand adventure."

The officer nodded, jotting down her words. "Did they say where they were heading?"

The waitress shook her head. "No, but they met with Dr. Bellamy before leaving. They all looked pretty serious about something."

The mention of Dr. Bellamy sent ripples through the department; her reputation as a historian was well-known, and it didn't take long for officers to connect the dots between her expertise and the mysterious diary that Rebecca inherited.

At the solitary news hub in Wollow Creek, machines buzzed energetically while journalists assembled a narrative destined to enthrall the populace. Dominating the front page was the bold title: "Community Youths Vanish – Spotted With Renowned Scholar." The accompanying story detailed the final confirmed sighting of Rebecca and Isaac and meticulously described Dr. Bellamy's transport—a deep green sport utility vehicle marked by a unique indentation on its back bumper.

A television crew descended upon the municipality to report on the vanished group, further stirring excitement within the community.

Rumours swirled around town as neighbours speculated over cups of coffee and pastries. Some spoke of ancient curses and daring quests; others worried about more mundane dangers that might have befallen the young adventurers.

Across town, at Wollow Creek Police Station, officers huddled around a map marked with sightings and tips from locals. Each report brought them closer to pinpointing the trio's route.

"We've got a possible sighting at a campsite two towns over," one officer announced, tapping a finger on a circled area of the map. "Witnesses say they saw Dr. Bellamy's SUV parked there overnight."

Another officer piped up from his desk near the window. "Gas station attendant over on Route 7 said he saw them stocking up on supplies yesterday evening."

With each new piece of information, excitement buzzed through the room; they were closing in on Rebecca, Isaac, and Dr. Bellamy's trail.

As dusk settled over Wollow Creek, police cruisers sped along winding roads leading out of town. Their lights pierced through gathering fog as officers remained vigilant for any sign of Dr. Bellamy's green SUV.

Little did they know that miles away, under cover of dense forest canopy, three figures huddled around a campfire—their eyes reflecting determination mixed with apprehension as they planned their next move under starlit skies.

Under a sky scattered with stars, the crackle of the campfire played accompaniment to laughter and tales. Rebecca, her eyes reflecting the dance of flames, shared a story of her great-grandmother Eleanor's encounter with a mischievous raccoon during a picnic that turned into an unexpected game of hide and seek with nature's own bandit. Isaac, leaning back on his palms, chuckled at the memory of a childhood camping trip where he'd mistaken a skunk for a cat, much to his olfactory dismay.

Dr. Bellamy, adjusting her glasses as if to see their pasts more clearly, regaled them with an anecdote from her early days in archaeology, when she'd confidently translated an ancient inscription only to realize she'd inadvertently praised the local donkey instead of the revered historical figure. Their laughter rose and fell like the embers soaring into the night.

In that fleeting moment, Rebecca experienced a rare sense of being truly understood, her quiet demeanor enveloped by the comforting embrace of shared connection and understanding. Isaac's laughter echoed with a timbre of newfound ease, his initial reluctance dissolving in the shared glow of camaraderie. Dr. Bellamy's scholarly demeanour softened as she contributed her own missteps to their collection of stories.

They were worlds away from the concern that gripped Wollow Creek—a concern plastered on posters and splashed across television screens. Unbeknownst to them, their faces were now familiar to strangers in towns they had never set foot in.

Morning brought with it dew-laden grass and an air crisp with possibility. The trio packed their campsite with practiced efficiency, eager to resume their quest. They drove through another town nestled between rolling hills and drowsy storefronts, where Rebecca caught sight of something that sent a jolt through her spine—a poster bearing three all-too-familiar faces.

She tapped Isaac's shoulder, pointing wordlessly at their own images plastered next to words like "MISSING" and "LAST SEEN." Dr. Bellamy slowed the SUV to a crawl as they all stared at the poster in silence. Dr. Bellamy removing her glasses, cleaning them as if clarity could change what they saw.

"We have to be careful," Dr. Bellamy muttered under her breath as she guided the SUV down less conspicuous streets.

Rebecca folded into herself, thoughts racing. The reality of their situation pressed down on her like a physical weight—their journey now not just an adventure but a flight from misunderstanding and misplaced worry.

Dr. Bellamy turned to face them both from the drivers seat. "We need to avoid attention," she said calmly. "We'll continue as planned but with discretion."

Their journey took on a new dimension—a delicate dance between discovery and secrecy—as they navigated through towns and landscapes under the cover of anonymity.

Elsewhere, eyes as dark as ravines cloaked in shadows narrowed at the newspaper's article. Anton Kozlov's finger, which had dug through soil for countless treasures, traced the photographs. He was not driven by concern or curiosity but by greed—a hunger for power he believed would be satisfied by gaining a treasure like the Amulet.

Hearing about the trio's quest; his ambition did not include sharing or unity but domination and control. Kozlov packed his gear with methodical precision—tools of trade for one who would pry secrets from the earth and hoard them like a dragon its gold.

He'd heard whispers of missing amulets, snatches of legend that spoke of curses and hidden power—a power he intended to wield for himself. Kozlov set out with an unshakeable resolve; his pursuit was not one of self-discovery but acquisition.

Unbeknownst to the trio, their journey pressed forward, each step drawing them deeper into the unknown. Little did they realize, they were no longer solitary in their quest. From the shadows, unseen eyes tracked their movements with a malevolent intent, their gaze as piercing as the void between stars, casting an ominous shadow over the path that lay ahead.

⸺ ❖ ⸻

Dirt smeared across our faces, as the trail behind us lay scattered with fleeting shadows. Isaac, Dr. Bellamy, and I had been eluding capture for days, our likenesses resonating from every town's announcement planks. Concealed at the back of a diner, we huddled close, heads bowed as though plotting our next move.

"We need to become ghosts," Isaac muttered, his eyes scanning the faces in the greasy spoon. "Invisible."

Dr. Bellamy pushed her glasses up her nose, her brain ticking like a clock. "We could alter our appearances—haircuts, clothing swaps, perhaps even a change in posture and gait."

My fingers toyed with the edge of the map spread between us. "What if we take it further? We could pick up some theatrical makeup. If we're going to hide in plain sight, we might as well go all out."

Isaac's eyes lit up like firecrackers. "That's brilliant, Bec. Let's make ourselves unrecognizable."

And so we did. Dr. Bellamy chopped her dark hair to shoulder length and donned a vibrant scarf that hid her features. Isaac shaved his sandy blond hair down to stubble and adopted a slouch that shaved inches off his height. I smeared freckles across my nose and cheeks with makeup and swapped my pendant for chunky, distracting jewellery.

We emerged from the bathroom transformed: a trio of strangers even mirrors would question.

As we drove away from that diner, I noticed something change in the air between us—a shift as subtle as the twilight merging into night.

Dr. Bellamy broke the silence first, her voice a soft hum in the SUV's cabin. "You know, this amulet... I believe it represents something more than just an artifact or a piece of history."

Isaac nodded; his hands steady on the wheel. "It's like it's calling us to become part of something bigger than ourselves."

I gazed out at the rolling hills passing by. "Maybe it's about connection—how we're all linked across time and space."

Dr. Bellamy adjusted her scarf thoughtfully. "It might be a symbol of healing too—mending broken lines, bridging gaps between generations."

We mulled over this in companionable silence until the road before us yawned into evening.

As stars pricked holes in the fabric of night, Isaac parked off-road beside an ancient oak whose limbs whispered secrets to the wind.

"Hey," he said, after Dr. Bellamy had settled into her tent for the night.

I turned to him; his blue eyes held a gravity I hadn't seen before.

"I need to tell you why I was hesitant about this... all of this." He took a deep breath that seemed to draw from wells deep within him.

"When I was little," he began, voice barely above a whisper, "my dad left on an expedition much like this one—chasing some myth across continents." He paused, swallowing hard against memories that clawed their way up his throat.

"He never came back." His words fell heavy between us.

My heart clenched for him—a pain so acute it was almost my own. "Isaac..."

He shook his head as if to clear it of ghosts. "I made myself a promise then—to never get caught up in such fairy tales." A bitter smile touched his lips.

"But then you showed up with that diary," he continued, his gaze locked on mine, "and something about your conviction... It stirred up old dreams I thought I'd buried deep."

His confession hung in the air like mist over morning meadows.

"I'm sorry," I murmured, the words escaping my lips like a fragile whisper after what felt like an eternity of heavy silence.

"Don't be." He exhaled slowly as if releasing chains that had bound him for years. "This journey—it's helping me face those demons... And who knows?" He offered me a wry grin that didn't quite reach his eyes but held more warmth than before.

"Maybe we'll find more than just an amulet at the end of all this."

Chapter 5

We had been on the road for nearly five days, the SUV eating miles of asphalt, then gravel, then nothing but dust. Our journey led us through towns that clung to the map with a stubborn dot, through mountains that rose like the spines of slumbering giants, down dirt roads that seemed to unravel from beneath our wheels. We'd suffered two flat tires—each a testament to our persistence. Isaac cussed and sweated over each one while Dr. Bellamy provided commentary on the local geology or history, her voice an odd comfort amid the trials.

Now, as we rumbled into a wide valley cradled by ancient hills, I could feel the palpable shift in the air. The map in Jeremiah's journal lay open on my lap, his meticulous scrawl a guidepost to something more than just a location—a gateway to the past.

We came to a stop at what appeared to be the end of any recognizable trail. Here was where we would begin our true journey, not just over land but through time itself.

I stepped out of the SUV and surveyed our surroundings. The valley was a tapestry of shadows and whispers; ruins peppered the landscape like forgotten memories made stone. Pillars stood as silent sentinels over what was once a thriving settlement. Walls crumbled under the weight of centuries, their stories reduced to rubble and overgrown vegetation.

"We're here," I announced, my voice barely above a whisper as if afraid to disturb the spirits that might linger.

Dr. Bellamy emerged from the vehicle, her eyes alight with curiosity and reverence. "Can you feel it?" she murmured. "The weight of history is heavy here."

Isaac nodded, his usual bravado tempered by awe. "It's like stepping into another world."

The three of us shouldered our packs and began our trek into this realm of antiquity. Our footsteps echoed against stone as we navigated narrow pathways that snaked between ruins. We traversed canyons whose walls held echoes of ancient laughter and cries; we scaled mountains that challenged us with steep ascents and precarious drops.

Jeremiah's journal became our oracle as we sought direction from its age-worn pages. His instructions led us deeper into this forgotten place where modernity's grip loosened with each step.

It was midday when we encountered our first true test—a puzzle Jeremiah indicated in his writings.

In a small clearing encircled by towering trees and stone fragments, we found an arrangement of boulders etched with symbols that matched those in the journal.

Dr. Bellamy knelt beside them, tracing her fingers over the cold stone carvings. "These symbols... they're not merely decorative," she mused aloud. "They're a language."

Isaac leaned over her shoulder, his gaze following her movements. "Yeah, but what are they saying?"

I unfolded another section of Jeremiah's journal and held it out for them to see—a page filled with similar symbols accompanied by notes in Jeremiah's hand.

"It's a riddle," I concluded after studying his notes.

Dr. Bellamy stood up abruptly, excitement coloring her tone. "Of course! The symbols represent elements—earth, air, fire, water."

Isaac arched an eyebrow. "So what? We gonna start bending them like some cartoon characters?"

I chuckled despite myself but shook my head. "No, look here." I pointed at Jeremiah's notes where he correlated each symbol with a natural feature of this very valley—a rocky outcrop for earth, a gap between cliffs for air, a dried-up riverbed for water...

"And fire?" Isaac prompted when I fell silent.

I glanced around until my eyes landed on a blackened patch of earth some distance away—a site once scorched by flame.

"We need to align ourselves with these elements," Dr. Bellamy surmised. "Perhaps position ourselves in relation to each symbol."

It took us the better part of an hour under the relentless sun to find our respective places—me at earth's stone embrace, Isaac standing tall where air danced through an invisible corridor between cliffs, Dr. Bellamy in the parched riverbed with pebbles that once knew water's caress.

"Nothing's happening," Isaac called out after several long moments had passed.

I checked Jeremiah's journal again and then it hit me—the solution wasn't just about positioning; it was about unity and balance among elements.

"Join hands!" I shouted across the clearing.

We rushed toward each other until our hands met in the center of the symbols—my dusty palm against Isaac's calloused grip and Dr. Bellamy's slender fingers completing our circle.

A low rumble vibrated beneath our feet as if the valley itself responded to Jeremiah's riddle being solved after all these years.

Our joined hands trembled—not from fear but from an exhilarating sense of connection with one another and with something much larger than ourselves—as we waited for whatever came next on this path laid out before us by history's indomitable will.

whatever came next on this path laid out before us by history's indomitable will.

Our voyage persisted, and we approached the subsequent obstacle; the towering stone barriers of the dilapidated structure overshadowed us, their formidable engravings now faint murmurs of a distant past. Tracing the indentations with my fingertips, I sensed the remnants of antiquity vibrating under my skin. We found ourselves at what seemed an impasse in our quest, confronted by a chamber hermetically closed off by an unyielding door. Decorated with icons and inscriptions, it stood like a custodian over mysteries reserved for deserving spirits.

Isaac scrutinized the barrier with a furrowed brow, his hands idly toying with a small gadget he had brought along. Dr. Bellamy, her eyes shielded behind those ever-present glasses, poured over Jeremiah's journal with a scholar's fervor.

"It's no use," Isaac muttered, pocketing the device. "There's no mechanical way through this."

Dr. Bellamy looked up from the journal, adjusting her glasses as if to refocus on the present challenge. "This isn't about mechanics," she said with calm authority. "It's about understanding. These symbols—they're not just decorative. They're a message."

I stepped closer to the door, eyes tracing the intricate patterns that seemed to dance before me. "What kind of message?" I asked.

Dr. Bellamy approached, her finger hovering over the glyphs as she translated. "It speaks of balance and harmony—of opening oneself to the past to unlock the future."

Isaac joined us, leaning in to study the door more closely. "Harmony, huh? So we need to figure out how these symbols relate to each other?"

"Precisely," Dr. Bellamy affirmed.

The symbols were arranged in pairs across the door's surface. I noticed that some were worn more than others, suggesting frequent contact. "Maybe it's like an instrument," I mused aloud. "Each symbol could be a note, and together they play a melody that opens the door."

Dr. Bellamy's eyes sparkled with interest at my suggestion. "Rebecca might be onto something."

"Okay," Isaac said, rolling up his sleeves. "Let's find this tune."

Together we examined each symbol pair, trying different combinations of pressure and sequence like musicians tuning their instruments before a concert. Time slipped by unnoticed as we worked in unison, frustration mounting with each failed attempt.

Finally, Dr. Bellamy stepped back, her gaze sweeping over us both before resting on me. "Rebecca, you have an ear for patterns—something neither Isaac nor I possess in quite the same way." She gestured toward the door with an encouraging nod.

Taking a deep breath, I closed my eyes and reached out to touch the symbols again, focusing on their individual resonances rather than their visual forms. My fingertips glided from one glyph to another as if drawn by an unseen force.

"There," I whispered more to myself than to my companions as I pressed two opposing symbols simultaneously.

A low rumble vibrated through the chamber as the stone door began to slide open with agonizing slowness, revealing another passage veiled in darkness.

Isaac let out a low whistle of appreciation while Dr. Bellamy clapped her hands together softly in applause.

"Brilliant work!" she exclaimed.

I smiled sheepishly at their praise, but beneath the surface, a warm sense of pride swelled within me. I had played a vital role in our quest, and knowing that filled me with a sense of accomplishment unlike any other.

With flashlights drawn and excitement fueling our steps, we ventured into the newly revealed corridor.

Our journey continued deeper into the ruins where hallways twisted and turned like serpents in slumber until we came upon our next challenge—a room where walls were lined with ancient text and symbols unfamiliar even to Dr. Bellamy's trained eye.

"These are older... much older than anything we've seen so far," she said while inspecting them closely.

"Any idea what language this is?" Isaac asked, his gaze darting between Dr. Bellamy and me.

"It might be proto-Indo-European roots mixed with local dialects... It will take time to translate."

Isaac rummaged through his backpack and pulled out an odd assortment of items: a magnifying glass, some string, chalk dust...

"How can this help?" I asked curiously.

He grinned at me—a flash of mischief in his eyes—and tied one end of the string around a small stick he'd picked up along our path earlier that day. "We make our own tools," he said confidently.

While Dr. Bellamy worked on deciphering the text with her scholarly expertise and Isaac improvised tools for closer inspection or reaching high-placed inscriptions, I took a step back to survey our surroundings as a whole.

Observing them both at work—Dr. Bellamy's mind unraveling linguistic knots and Isaac's hands deftly crafting makeshift aids—I realized that while each of us brought unique skills to our quest, it was my role to weave them together into cohesive action.

"Dr. B," I called firmly enough for both of them to pause and listen, "Can you focus on sections that repeat? There might be a common phrase or invocation."

"And Isaac," I continued while pointing toward one particularly high section of text only faintly visible in our flashlight beams, "can you use your contraption there to make rubbings? It might help Dr. B compare texts visually."

As they nodded in agreement and set back to work with renewed vigor under my direction, I couldn't help but feel that perhaps this was what Eleanor saw in me—a leader not by loud command but by guiding others toward their strengths and knitting together their talents like threads in a tapestry.

Hours melded into one another as Dr. Bellamy pieced together translations and Isaac captured every nuance of the high inscriptions until finally...

"I think I have it," Dr. Bellamy announced triumphantly yet breathlessly from her exhaustive efforts.

Isaac and I rushed over as she recited an incantation—a call for wisdom from ancestors long passed—and at her words' conclusion...

The floor beneath us shuddered before slowly descending into darkness below like an ancient elevator activated by forgotten knowledge spoken anew—a path leading onward toward secrets waiting patiently for those brave enough to seek them out.

The sun commenced its downward journey behind the lofty escarpments, projecting elongated silhouettes that stretched finger-like over the terrain. Guided by the map, our route dipped beneath, tracing the erratic penmanship of Jeremiah that wove among venerable boulders, murmuring of bygone eras. The evening's coolness sharply differed from the daytime warmth, prompting me to draw my jacket closer as we neared the mouth of a slender cavern..

Isaac adjusted his backpack, his eyes scanning the map and then the landscape with a navigator's precision. "This is it," he murmured, more to himself than to us. Dr. Bellamy nodded, her gaze locked on the yawning mouth of darkness before us.

Summoning my courage, I took a step forward, my fingers instinctively finding the pendant nestled against my chest. Its cool touch against my skin served as an anchor, grounding me in the moment as we braced ourselves to descend into the depths below. With each beat of my heart, I felt Eleanor's presence, her spirit infusing me with strength and resolve, guiding my every step into the unknown.

As we moved forward, I sensed eyes upon us—watchful and curious. The locals from a nearby village had taken an interest in our presence since we arrived at the site. Their whispers were a low hum behind us, their steps discreet yet unmistakable as they followed at a cautious distance.

Isaac caught my eye, his brow furrowed with concern. "We've got company," he said.

Dr. Bellamy glanced over her shoulder and sighed. "Let's hope they're just curious about outsiders."

The cave entrance stood before us like a gaping maw, its darkness threatening to swallow us whole. With a final glance at the sky above, I steeled myself and stepped into the cavern, the cool embrace of underground air washing over my face like a whispered promise of mysteries awaiting discovery.

Our footsteps echoed off the walls as we made our way deeper into the cave. The locals' presence was an unspoken tension among us, their curiosity palpable in every shuffled step behind us.

Suddenly, Isaac stopped short, holding up his hand for us to halt. A man from the village stepped forward into our dim circle of light. His face was etched with lines of suspicion and something that resembled fear.

"Why do you come here?" he asked in accented English, his voice echoing off the stone walls.

Dr. Bellamy took a step forward, her voice calm and steady. "We're historians and explorers," she explained. "We're following a trail left by an ancestor."

The man's eyes narrowed at her words. "This place is sacred to us," he said. "Not for outsiders to trample."

Beside me, I sensed Isaac tense, his unease palpable like a storm brewing beneath calm waters, threatening to erupt into a tempest that could engulf us all.

Stepping forward, I cleared my throat. The pendant seemed to thrum against my chest—a silent heartbeat urging me on.

"We mean no disrespect," I said gently. "My great-great-grandfather loved these lands just as you do. We only wish to learn from them—to honor his memory."

The man looked at me for a long moment before his gaze dropped to the pendant swinging lightly from my neck.

"That... it belonged to your elder?" His voice softened as he gestured towards it.

I nodded eagerly, encouraged by his interest. "Yes, it was my great-grandmother's," I replied. "She taught me to cherish our history and respect traditions."

A murmur rippled through the group of locals gathered behind him—a mix of curiosity and something that sounded like approval.

"You carry her spirit," he said after a pause that stretched like taut wire between two cliffs.

As Isaac's hand settled on my shoulder, a silent gesture of solidarity, I drew strength from his presence, his support a comforting anchor in the midst of uncertainty. Dr. Bellamy's approving glance conveyed a reassurance that resonated deep within me, igniting a flicker of confidence that burned brightly despite the looming shadows of doubt.

"We seek only knowledge," Dr. Bellamy added respectfully, "and understanding."

The man studied each of our faces in turn before finally stepping aside with a slow nod. The tension broke like a wave against rocks, leaving behind a cautious truce.

"Be mindful," he warned with a gravity that weighed heavily in the air. "The spirits are watching."

With his permission granted in hushed tones and nods from his companions, we continued our descent into darkness below—the map leading us forward into unknown depths where history lay buried beneath layers of time and dust.

As we delved deeper into the caverns, our only companions the beams of our flashlights piercing through the suffocating darkness, an unsettling sensation gripped me. It wasn't just the eyes of curious locals I felt upon us, but the weight of something ancient and primal—a presence that stirred in the depths, watching with eyes older than any living soul above ground.

With each step I took in the company of Isaac and Dr. Bellamy—my steadfast friends and allies—I felt a surge of confidence rising within me, swelling like a tide. It wasn't just confidence in my own abilities, but in the strength of our collective resolve, in our shared purpose, and in the journey that lay ahead of us. Together, we were more than the sum of our parts, and that realization buoyed my spirits, driving away the shadows of doubt that threatened to encroach upon our path.

The walls whispered secrets of an age long forgotten as we descended into the earth's belly, our torches flickering like the hesitant heartbeats of intrepid explorers trespassing in time's sacred vault. Dr. Bellamy's shadow loomed over ancient scripts etched into the stone, her fingers tracing the grooves with scholarly reverence. Isaac and I exchanged glances, the weight of anticipation pressing upon us like the earthen ceiling above.

"It's here," Dr. Bellamy murmured, her voice a reverent hush amidst the quietude of history.

Her announcement jolted Isaac and me into heightened alertness. I moved nearer, breaths catching in my throat. Atop a pedestal hewn from the solid rock rested a stone tablet adorned with an unusual pattern of symbols – consulting the journal, it seemed to be yet another enigma.

Isaac peered closer, his gaze intense with concentration. "Seems to be a type of combination lock," he observed, his hands eager for contact.

Dr. Bellamy raised a hand. "Be wary," she cautioned. "Jeremiah advised that this challenge would be neither straightforward nor benign."

With the journal as our guide, we studied the cryptic clues left by my great-great-grandfather. The symbols were a language unto themselves, one that spoke of lineage and legacy—a riddle only his blood could unravel.

My heart raced as I reached out tentatively toward the slab, my fingers hovering above it. The symbols beckoned me: a crescent moon, a sunburst, an open eye. They seemed to glow under my touch as I pressed them in sequence—Jeremiah's secret sequence.

A grinding noise reverberated through the chamber as gears hidden within ancient mechanisms turned with begrudging compliance. A section of the wall receded with a groan before sliding aside to reveal a cavity within the rock.

We crowded around the newly revealed compartment, peering inside to discover its contents—a metal fragment, intricately designed and humming with an energy that resonated through my very bones.

"The first piece," Isaac breathed out, disbelief mingling with awe in his voice.

Dr. Bellamy reached in with trembling hands to retrieve it carefully from its resting place. The metal was cool to the touch yet seemed to thrum with life as if recognizing that it had been found and was ready to be awakened from its long slumber.

"It's beautiful," I whispered, barely trusting myself to speak lest I shatter the moment like glass underfoot.

Isaac gave a mute nod, his gaze not only catching the flicker of torchlight but also mirroring the reawakened blaze of victory and exploration, even as fatigue was evident, compelling him to collect his breath.

We gathered around our prize; three disparate souls bound by purpose and now by success. The piece was smaller than I had imagined but its presence was immense—as if we held not just metal but condensed history in our hands.

Dr. Bellamy handled it with reverence fit for a sacred relic; her face etched with both wonder and concern. "Do you realize what this means?" she asked us softly.

I nodded slowly; comprehension dawning on me like sunrise on new snow—the amulet was real, our quest tangible now more than ever before.

Isaac, struggling to catch his breath, swept his hand through his hair—an act that morphed from frustration to disbelief and finally to acceptance. "We're actually doing this," he uttered, the spoken words seeming to solidify the reality of their endeavor.

"We are," I confirmed, my voice echoing with a resolve that belied the tremors of uncertainty coursing through me.

The moment lingered—suspended like dust motes caught in sunlight—before Dr. Bellamy cleared her throat firmly enough to break our collective reverie.

"While this is indeed an incredible discovery," she began, "we must be aware that artifacts such as these can be... unpredictable."

Her words hung in the air—ominous and true—as she turned the amulet piece over in her hands with careful scrutiny.

"Unpredictable how?" Isaac asked, ever eager for knowledge despite potential peril.

"Powerful objects can have powerful protectors... or seekers," Dr. Bellamy explained. "This piece may have been hidden away for good reason—not just to protect it from those who would use it for ill but perhaps also because its power is not fully understood."

Her words sent a shiver down my spine, the stark reminder of danger lurking ahead causing a surge of conflicting emotions to stir within me. While excitement for the adventure ahead pulsed through my veins, it was now tempered by the cold grip of fear, as the fantasies of Jeremiah's tales gave way to the harsh reality of our present journey.

"And there's more than just physical danger," she continued. "There are ethical considerations when dealing with such potent history."

I pondered her words—my great-great-grandfather's quest wasn't just about breaking curses or proving worth; it was about responsibility toward history itself.

"We need to tread carefully," Dr. Bellamy finished.

As we stood in the chamber, a chill seemed to settle over us, permeating the air with an icy intensity. Yet, I couldn't help but wonder if the sudden drop in temperature was merely a reflection of our own cooling nerves, our adrenaline-fueled excitement giving way to a sobering sense of accountability. We were no longer just adventurers chasing thrills; we were guardians of truth, accountable not only to ourselves but to the secrets we sought to uncover.

The echo of our ascent back towards daylight was contemplative—a silent agreement among us that while we had triumphed today, tomorrow held no promises save for uncertainty and the weighty responsibility of those who dare disturb slumbering secrets nestled within earth's embrace.

Chapter 6

O ur collective sense of wonder was palpable as we gazed upon the Amulet's initial fragment, the once fanciful stories Eleanor regaled us with now tangibly woven into the fabric of our existence.

With an air of scholarly intrigue, Dr. Bellamy inclined her head forward, the lenses of her spectacles magnifying the awe in her eyes. "Remarkable," she breathed out, the soft reverberation of her astonishment gently playing off the ancient stone walls that encased us.

Isaac flashed a grin that couldn't hide the shadow of concern in his eyes. "One down," he said, clapping a hand on my shoulder, "who knows how many to go."

I nodded, turning to the journal again. The pages were brittle with age, but Jeremiah's handwriting was meticulous—a clear path penned across time. The next direction beckoned us to another part of the world entirely; it mentioned distant lands with cryptic clues entwined within history and legend.

Delving into my bag, I retrieved the envelope labeled "For the Trip." However, as I counted the bills within, a pang of unease gripped me. The amount felt painfully insufficient for the scope of our ambitious journey spanning continents. My mind buzzed with a flurry of calculations and logistical concerns, grappling with the daunting reality of navigating unknown territories and facing unforeseen dangers.

We gathered around an old wooden table Isaac had set up outside our makeshift campsite. Dr. Bellamy cleared her throat, adjusting her glasses as if preparing for a lecture. "We must plan carefully," she began. "Our resources are finite, and we're venturing into unknown territory."

Isaac unfolded a map across the table, his finger tracing possible routes. "We've got to be smart about this," he said. "Transportation's going to be tricky without drawing attention."

I bit my lip, looking from one to the other. They were right; this was bigger than any of us had anticipated. Yet Eleanor had entrusted me with this quest—she believed in me when no one else did.

"I know it seems overwhelming," I admitted, meeting their gazes. "But we've made it this far together." My voice grew steadier with each word. "We can't back down now—not when we're starting to uncover Jeremiah's legacy."

Dr. Bellamy nodded slowly, respect flickering in her eyes. "The historical significance alone is staggering," she mused.

Isaac's lips twitched into a smile as he met my gaze again. "Plus," he added with his characteristic charm, "turning back now would make for one boring story."

We laughed together—a brief respite from the gravity of our situation—and then buckled down to brass tacks.

"We'll need to be economical with our funds," Dr. Bellamy pointed out pragmatically.

I chimed in with newfound confidence. "Maybe we can reach out to contacts from your museum? Scholars or historians who might be willing to help?"

Isaac ran a hand through his sandy hair thoughtfully. "And I've got some buddies who might not mind bending rules for a good cause—or at least turning a blind eye for a quick favor."

Our conversation flowed seamlessly into action plans and contingency arrangements—routes plotted out on maps that crisscrossed over oceans and mountains; contacts listed with notes on potential assistance; strategies devised for evading both authorities and Anton Kozlov's relentless pursuit.

As night fell and stars blinked into existence above us, something unspoken yet palpable shifted between us—a recognition that this journey was shaping us as much as we were navigating it.

"I'm in this for the long haul," Isaac declared after a stretch of silence.

Dr. Bellamy gave him an approving nod before turning her attention to me. "Rebecca," she said with an intensity that demanded full attention, "your great-grandmother saw something extraordinary in you—and so do we."

Her words warmed me from within like nothing else could have at that moment—validation from someone I respected so deeply made all my fears seem smaller somehow.

Summoning courage from the depths of my being, I drew in a deep breath before uttering words that had long remained unspoken: "I've spent so much of my life feeling invisible." Though my voice trembled with the weight of vulnerability, it remained steadfast, fortified by the unwavering support of my trusted allies. "But now... now I feel like I'm part of something important—with you guys by my side."

We exchanged smiles that carried more weight than any spoken promise could—each one an unbreakable vow forged in adventure and illuminated by starlight.

"Let's do this—for Eleanor, for Jeremiah, and for ourselves," I concluded.

Isaac nodded solemnly while Dr. Bellamy placed her hand over mine—a silent gesture of solidarity.

As we sat there under the cloak of nightfall, surrounded by ancient whispers and timeless secrets, our bond cemented into something unshakeable—a trio bound by purpose and strengthened by mutual trust.

With our commitment renewed and spirits buoyed by each other's resolve, we agreed to rise with dawn's first light—each step forward bringing us closer not just to pieces of an amulet but also toward discovering pieces of ourselves along this journey of self-discovery and historic revelation.

We had ventured far from the comforting embrace of Wollow Creek, its familiar streets now just a memory cradled in the back of my mind. Here, in the vastness of open land, we had only each other and the journey that stretched out before us like an unrolled scroll. Law enforcement was a distant concern now; their search radius couldn't stretch to the remote corners we found ourselves in.

Yet, despite the distance we'd put between us and any immediate threat from home, a shiver skated down my spine as I caught Isaac casting nervous glances over his shoulder. Dr. Bellamy seemed absorbed in her notes, her brow furrowed as if she were trying to decode an invisible message etched between the lines.

"You okay?" I asked Isaac.

He nodded but didn't meet my gaze. "Just thought I saw something move back there."

Dr. Bellamy looked up from her papers. "Probably just a local curious about our presence," she said, though her voice lacked conviction.

As dusk descended, its fiery orange and muted violet hues enveloping the horizon in a breathtaking embrace, we hastily pitched camp, preparing for the imminent arrival of nightfall. As darkness began to assert its dominion, casting long shadows across our makeshift sanctuary, we huddled around the crackling campfire, seeking solace and shared warmth in its flickering glow. Yet, despite Isaac's valiant efforts to lighten the mood with his spirited tales, an unsettling sensation lingered in the air—a haunting feeling that we were not alone, that unseen eyes watched our every move from the depths of the surrounding wilderness.

The night passed without incident, though sleep was a restless affair for me. At dawn's break, we packed up silently, each lost in their thoughts as we continued on our path.

I noticed then that our trail was marked by more than just our footprints; others had treaded here recently. A jolt of alarm coursed through me when I spotted boot prints intermingled with ours — too large to belong to any of us.

Dr. Bellamy noticed my gaze and followed it to the ground. Her lips pressed into a thin line.

"We need to be cautious," she murmured. "Whoever is following us knows what they're doing."

The day wore on under a watchful sun as we trekked toward our next destination outlined in Jeremiah's journal. The terrain grew more challenging, and so did my thoughts — swirling with possibilities about who could be tailing us and why.

Our shadows stretched long when we finally settled for another night's rest at the edge of a sleepy village whose lights flickered like distant stars. We kept our camp discreet this time, hidden from prying eyes by a thicket of trees.

In hushed tones, we discussed our plan for the next day over a sparse meal when Dr. Bellamy paused mid-sentence.

"Do you hear that?" she whispered.

The crackling fire seemed to hush at her words, and I strained my ears against the silence that followed. There it was — faint murmurs carrying on the wind from the direction of the village.

Isaac reached for his makeshift weapon — a hefty branch he'd taken to carrying — and I admired his instinct to protect even though my heart raced with fear.

"We're not equipped for confrontation," Dr. Bellamy said. "Let's hope it doesn't come to that."

In silent accord, we divided the night into shifts, a tacit acknowledgment passing between us that something ominous loomed on the horizon. Though unspoken, the weight of anticipation hung heavy in the air, a collective understanding that our vigilance was paramount. As each of us took our turn to stand guard, the night enveloped us in an eerie stillness, broken only by the crackling of the dwindling fire and the rustle of unseen creatures in the surrounding darkness.

My turn at watch was last, and as dawn teased the edges of night away, I caught sight of a figure at the periphery of our camp — someone observing us with keen interest before slipping away into the waking village.

We packed up quickly once Isaac and Dr. Bellamy woke up; there was no time to waste with an unknown threat lurking so close by.

As we approached the village for supplies under the guise of mere travelers passing through, Isaac's grip on his branch tightened beside me.

"You think they're here?" he muttered under his breath so only I could hear.

"Someone is," I replied just as quietly.

The villagers we encountered were few in number, yet their warmth and hospitality were palpable, their smiles genuine as they shared directions and tales of local lore. However, amidst the friendly faces, one man stood out, his gaze piercing and unsettling, as if his eyes bore into the depths of my soul whenever they met ours across the bustling market square.

Dr. Bellamy's keen intuition must have sensed the unease that permeated the air, for she wasted no time in guiding us away from the unsettling man with a sense of urgency thinly veiled beneath her composed exterior. Once we had obtained what we needed from the market, she deftly steered us clear of his penetrating gaze, leading us down winding alleys and through narrow streets until we were safely out of his sight.

It wasn't until later that day when we were safely away from prying eyes that she revealed what she'd overheard while bartering for supplies: hushed conversations spoken in local dialect about outsiders seeking powerful relics; whispers about a man named Anton Kozlov who paid well for information about such endeavors.

My blood ran cold at his name — Kozlov, the treasure hunter whose reputation for ruthlessness preceded him like a shadow stretching far ahead on sunless days.

"He's closer than we thought," Dr. Bellamy said as we found solace under an outcrop that shielded us from view on three sides.

"And he's not alone," Isaac added. "He's got locals on his payroll."

Our mission had been dangerous from its inception — I knew this much — but as reality dawned clearer than ever before under Dr. Bellamy's grave expression and Isaac's troubled frown, I understood: Our quest held stakes far higher than any amulet piece or family curse could measure.

We had become players in a game much larger than ourselves; pawns on a board where Kozlov seemed always two steps ahead.

———— • ◉ • • ————

We had been on the road for weeks, and the Jeep had become our makeshift home. The routine was simple: Isaac drove, Dr. Bellamy navigated with the journal and I took care of the camp each night. We fell into a rhythm, our actions choreographed by necessity and the unspoken understanding that grew between us.

Each dawn, Isaac assumed the responsibility of inspecting the SUV's oil levels and tire pressure, executing the task with the expertise of a trained mechanic. Dr. Bellamy would surface from her shelter, her tresses tousled yet her gaze sparkling with the excitement of our adventure. She'd reposition her spectacles and immerse herself once again in Jeremiah's journal, uttering remarks on historical frameworks and prospective clues.

As for me, I found solace in preparing our meals, something about the methodical process of chopping vegetables or brewing coffee brought me a sense of normalcy amidst the chaos of our journey. It was during these quiet moments that we would gather around our foldable table, discussing what we thought the power of the Austral Amulet could really be.

"The amulet's power must be profound," Dr. Bellamy would speculate, stirring her coffee absentmindedly. "Something that can foster unity and understanding? It's unlike any artifact I've studied before."

Isaac leaned back in his chair, casting a skeptical glance at the amulet piece nestled securely in its box. "What if it's just symbolic? You know, a representation of togetherness rather than some sort of magical force."

I considered their words carefully before responding. "Maybe it's both. Like how a flag can bring people together — it's not just the fabric that matters, but what it stands for."

We nodded collectively, comforted by the notion that we were chasing after something that could bring real change.

One evening as we set up camp under a sky peppered with stars, Dr. Bellamy attempted to pitch her tent with an air of confidence that quickly dissolved into frustration when the tent collapsed for the third time.

Isaac and I exchanged amused glances before joining her side.

"Here," Isaac said as he took one side of the tent from Dr. Bellamy's hands. "The trick is to secure this pole first."

I took hold of another part of the structure, anchoring it down as Isaac demonstrated his method to Dr. Bellamy.

"I must admit," she laughed self-deprecatingly, "my expertise in ancient cultures doesn't quite extend to modern camping equipment."

"Well," I chimed in with a smile, "we can't all be wilderness experts like Isaac here."

Isaac bowed mockingly, earning a chuckle from both of us.

From then on, Dr. Bellamy observed Isaac's technique closely, determined to master this new skill. Our light-hearted banter continued into dinner where Isaac revealed his less-than-culinary talents by burning what should have been simple toast.

"Perhaps history isn't your forte," Dr. Bellamy teased as she scraped blackened crumbs from her plate.

"I'll stick to driving and tents," Isaac retorted good-naturedly.

These moments—when laughter came easily and our burdens seemed lighter—were what kept us grounded.

As we continued on our journey each day brought its own challenges and wonders; every night offered time for reflection. Alone with my thoughts as I nestled into my sleeping bag one evening, I marveled at how much I had changed since leaving Wollow Creek.

At the outset of this journey, I had been tentative and uncertain, a mere shadow in the tapestry of my own life. However, amidst the unfolding saga of our quest for an ancient amulet—whether shrouded in myth or destined to reshape the world—I found myself truly seen. Not only by the unwavering support of Isaac and Dr. Bellamy but also by my own newfound clarity. Here, my decisions held weight, my voice resonated, and my actions were instrumental in shaping our collective fate. In the crucible of adventure, I discovered the power of my own agency, a revelation that illuminated the path ahead with newfound purpose and resolve.

Isaac had confided one evening that he'd felt stifled by the confines of Wollow Creek, ensnared by the weight of expectations and the monotony of small-town life. Yet, amidst the vast expanse of the open road, his true potential emerged. His resourcefulness proved invaluable, illuminating the path forward as we encountered challenges along our journey. Freed from the constraints of familiarity, Isaac thrived, his ingenuity serving as a guiding light through the unknown.

And Dr. Bellamy? She admitted once during an evening's discussion that her life had been all books and artifacts — solitary pursuits that lacked companionship like this. The journey had reminded her why she became a historian: not just to study history but to experience it firsthand — to feel it beneath her fingertips.

Together we were an unlikely trio bound by a common goal — each learning from each other and growing stronger because of it. Our camaraderie wasn't just born out of necessity but from genuine affection and respect that had blossomed over countless miles and shared experiences.

As I drifted off to sleep that night with their quiet breathing filling the tent, I knew no matter what lay ahead or what power the Austral Amulet held, this journey was already changing us all in ways we couldn't have imagined when we first set out from Wollow Creek.

Chapter 7

Arriving at our new destination by plane, dawn painted the horizon in hues of tangerine and rose as we approached the outskirts of an ancient city. A delicate mist swirled above cobblestone streets, like a veil gently lifted to reveal the splendor beneath. Buildings, aged and dignified, stood shoulder to shoulder, their facades adorned with intricate ironwork and weathered shutters that whispered stories of bygone eras. This was Cádiz, a historical port in Spain, where the whispers of Phoenicians, Romans, and Moors still echoed through the narrow alleys.

The air hummed with life, a symphony composed of chattering market vendors, the distant call of seagulls, and the soft lap of waves against the harbor walls. Vibrant awnings stretched over stalls brimming with sun-ripened fruit and fresh seafood, casting patterns on the stone below. Sunlight glanced off golden church domes while children played soccer in plazas framed by fountains carved from marble.

Dr. Bellamy led us through the maze of streets with an ease that spoke of her familiarity with places steeped in history. Isaac's keen eyes darted from one architectural marvel to another, his hand resting lightly on the wheel of his rugged backpack. I clutched Jeremiah's journal to my chest like a talisman, the weight of our mission grounding me amidst the sensory overload.

Our journey had brought us across oceans to seek the second piece of the Astral Amulet. Jeremiah's cryptic clues pointed us here, to this city where past and present danced in a lover's embrace.

But no adventure comes without its trials.

"El próximo tren a Sevilla... cancelado," droned the loudspeaker at the train station. Our heads swiveled toward each other as Dr. Bellamy translated.

"The next train to Seville is canceled."

Our collective sighs mingled with the ambient noise of travelers rushing about their business. Isaac ran a hand through his hair, exasperation evident on his face.

"Of course it is," he muttered. "What's our play now?"

We huddled around a metal bench, unfurling maps and scouring timetables with furrowed brows. Language wasn't just a barrier; it was an entire fortress wall we had yet to scale.

As Dr. Bellamy scanned the signs and notices posted around the station, her lips moved silently, deciphering the information before her. Isaac's gaze remained fixed on her, his expression intent as he observed her actions. After a moment, his attention drifted towards the window, where rows of taxis stood in regimented lines, their presence reminiscent of soldiers awaiting their next command.

"We could split up," he suggested. "One of us secures transportation while another figures out alternative routes."

Dr. Bellamy nodded in agreement but added a cautionary note.

"We should avoid drawing attention to ourselves."

I bit my lip, pondering our options when inspiration struck like lightning.

"Wait," I said, reaching into my bag for Eleanor's pendant necklace that I had kept hidden beneath my shirt since our departure from Wollow Creek. The intricate design seemed to glimmer with promise under the harsh fluorescent lights.

"Eleanor always said this was more than just jewelry; it was a compass for life." I let out a nervous chuckle as I unclasped it from around my neck and placed it on the map sprawled across our bench.

"What if it's not just metaphorical? What if it can actually guide us?"

Isaac raised an eyebrow but didn't dismiss my idea outright. Dr. Bellamy leaned forward, curiosity piqued as she studied the pendant.

With careful fingers, she rotated it over various points on the map until it settled over Seville—the city that held our next clue.

A faint but discernible pull tugged at my heartstrings as if Eleanor herself was nudging us onward.

"I have an idea," Dr. Bellamy said after a moment of contemplation. "There are local buses that run between towns; they're less likely to be affected by whatever has halted the trains."

Isaac's face brightened at her suggestion.

"And they're probably not looking for three travelers taking such an... unconventional route."

Our group split up as planned—I stayed behind to safeguard our belongings while Isaac ventured out to negotiate with taxi drivers for a ride to the nearest bus depot. Dr. Bellamy mingled among locals, gathering information with her broken but effective Spanish.

As I stood amidst the bustling station, time seemed to slip away like grains through an hourglass. Families embraced in joyful reunions, while lovers reluctantly parted ways, each moment a microcosm of life's perpetual cycle. Amidst the ebb and flow of human interactions, I couldn't help but feel a sense of awe at the intricate dance of emotions unfolding before me, a poignant reminder of the inexorable passage of time.

Finally, Isaac returned with good news—a taxi driver agreed to take us for a reasonable fare—and Dr. Bellamy confirmed there was indeed a bus that would carry us closer to our destination.

As we loaded our gear into the trunk of an old but sturdy taxi, I couldn't help but marvel at how we had transformed from strangers into allies bound by purpose and now into something more—a family forged through adversity.

We wove through Cádiz's heart one last time before breaking free from its embrace and heading toward rural landscapes that stretched toward Seville's promise.

Our makeshift family didn't need words as we journeyed onward; each one knew their role in this dance of destiny—Dr. Bellamy with her wisdom etched from years spent unearthing history's secrets; Isaac with his practical skills honed under Wollow Creek's vast skies; and me... finding my voice in Eleanor's echoes—a leader stepping into her legacy's light.

In this foreign land where every stone told a story, we wrote our own chapter—one filled with resilience and unity against uncertainty's tide.

Grime from the rough trail clung to our bodies, the creaking motor of a seasoned Jeep bearing witness to the numerous journeys it had made delivering travellers to their end points. The relentless sun, a blazing sphere in an unblemished sky, scorched us pitilessly. We had come to a land where the native speech moved to a cadence strange to our ears and the atmosphere was laden with the aromas of exotic spices and primeval soil.

Our arrival had stirred curiosity among the locals. Eyes followed our every move, whispers we couldn't understand floated through the air, and that's when she approached us—a figure with a presence that seemed to calm the whispers and settle the stares.

"Need some help?" Her voice was melodic, a soft breeze in the stifling heat.

Lila Martinez stood before us with an air of confidence that seemed rooted in the very soil we stood upon. She wore her long, curly black hair like a mantle of pride, her bright smile offering solace from our journey's fatigue.

"We might," I admitted, sharing a glance with Isaac and Dr. Bellamy.

Lila introduced herself as a local historian, her knowledge spanning generations of stories woven into the fabric of this place. Her eyes sparkled with intrigue as we explained our quest for the Austral Amulet.

"I know this land like the back of my hand," she said, gesturing toward the mountains that cradled the town. "And I've heard tales of your amulet since I was no taller than a cornstalk."

As Lila led us through narrow streets and bustling markets, she narrated tales of her ancestors—stories laced with courage and unity in diversity. Her words painted pictures of past battles fought on these lands and secret societies that protected ancient truths.

Dr. Bellamy listened intently, occasionally nodding or asking pointed questions about historical references that seemed to align with clues from Jeremiah's journal.

Isaac chipped in with logistical queries—safe places to rest, discreet paths to avoid unwanted attention. His eyes were alert; trust didn't come easy for him either.

As Lila wove her tales, I found myself captivated, hanging onto her every word. Her wisdom wasn't merely academic; it was infused with personal significance, passed down through generations like cherished heirlooms. Yet, amidst the richness of her storytelling, a seed of doubt took root within me.

As Lila delved into the tale of the hidden temple, weaving a narrative filled with mystery and intrigue, I felt a stirring within me. The legend held promises of hidden treasures and ancient secrets, but alongside my excitement, a sense of caution took root. Trust, like a foreign language to me, felt daunting and unfamiliar. While I recognized its importance, fluency eluded me, leaving me hesitant and uncertain in the face of Lila's revelations. Each word she spoke seemed to carry weight, each detail a potential clue or trap. As the story unfolded, I found myself teetering on the edge of belief and skepticism, unsure of where to place my trust in this world of legends and uncertainty.

The streets grew quieter as Lila guided us away from the center of town. We turned into an alley shadowed by overhanging balconies adorned with flowers and drying laundry.

"Rebecca?" Isaac's voice held an edge of concern.

I halted mid-step, my grip tightening on the strap of my bag where the first piece of the amulet rested against notebooks and maps.

"Something wrong?" Lila turned back toward us, her expression open and inviting trust.

My throat tightened as I tried to find words laced with enough diplomacy not to offend our guide yet still voice my apprehension.

"It's just—this is all so new," I started, hating how my voice trembled. "And we've got to be careful."

She nodded, understanding flashing in her eyes. "I get it," she said. "But you're not alone here."

Isaac stepped up beside me, his presence reassuring even if he didn't speak right away.

Dr. Bellamy adjusted her glasses before offering her input—a blend of reason and encouragement. "Rebecca has good instincts," she acknowledged, meeting my gaze with respect.

In that alleyway lined with cobblestones worn smooth by centuries of footsteps, I realized this journey was more than just about finding pieces of an amulet or breaking some family curse—it was about piecing together fragments of myself I didn't even know were missing.

I took a deep breath and nodded at Lila. "Lead on."

Her smile returned as she resumed guiding us through twists and turns until we reached an old building whose walls told stories in their cracks and vines.

"Here," Lila said as she pushed open an ornate wooden door that creaked on its hinges—a sound that seemed to echo through time itself.

Inside was cool relief from the heat outside—a haven filled with books, artifacts, and scrolls layered with dust and history.

"This is where you'll find your next clue," Lila declared, her words carrying a weight that transcended mere conviction; they resonated with a sense of destiny, as if ordained by forces beyond our comprehension.

Hours passed as we pored over ancient texts under Lila's guidance—her insights shedding light on cryptic passages from Jeremiah's journal.

As dusk settled like a soft blanket over the town outside, we found ourselves sharing stories over cups of steaming local brew—a blend so rich it seemed imbued with history itself.

Lila listened with rapt attention as Isaac reminisced about our childhood adventures in Wollow Creek, each memory feeling like a distant echo from another lifetime. With each anecdote, our shared past unfolded before us, a tapestry woven with threads of laughter and mischief.

Meanwhile, Dr. Bellamy regaled us with stories of her own, recounting dusty discoveries that had reshaped historical perspectives overnight. Her words carried the weight of ancient civilizations and forgotten secrets, painting a vivid picture of the mysteries waiting to be uncovered in the world beyond.

As my turn to share approached, a moment of hesitation gripped me tightly. The dreams that danced in the recesses of my mind, vast and untamed, seemed too grand to be voiced aloud. And yet, despite the daunting enormity of their magnitude, I summoned the courage to reveal them. With a heart laid bare, I dared to articulate the aspirations that often felt larger than life itself.

With a breath, I spoke of Eleanor's profound influence on my journey, her legacy shaping the very essence of who I aspired to become. In that vulnerable moment, I allowed fragments of my soul to unfurl, baring the depths of my desires and the yearning for a future that echoed with purpose and possibility.

Lila nodded along as if my dreams made perfect sense—to her they weren't flights of fancy but promises waiting to be fulfilled.

As night enveloped us in its embrace and stars began their timeless vigil overhead, I realized something had shifted within me—a tectonic plate moving so subtly yet profoundly under my identity's landscape.

Trust wasn't just about relying on others; it was about trusting myself—my decisions, my dreams... my journey.

⸻

The scent of antiquity hung thick in the air as our quartet approached the sunbaked stone archway. Lila, Isaac, Dr. Bellamy, and I had followed the worn map to a remote village where time seemed to stand still. We had arrived at what appeared to be an ancient library, its walls inscribed with fading glyphs that whispered secrets of a forgotten era.

"Look at this," Dr. Bellamy murmured, her finger tracing the contours of a carving. "It's not just decoration; it's a story."

I leaned closer, the pendant around my neck grazing the cool stone as I studied the intricate patterns. My great-great-grandfather's words echoed in my mind, urging me to look beyond the surface.

"It's about the harvest," Lila observed, her curls casting dancing shadows on the wall as she moved. "See how the figures are holding sheaves of grain?"

Isaac nodded, his sandy blond hair glinting in the sunlight that spilled through a crack in the ceiling. "But there's more to it," he said, pointing to a panel that depicted a celestial alignment. "These stars—they're not random.

They're constellations that would've been visible here at harvest time."

Dr. Bellamy adjusted her glasses and peered closer. "Isaac's right. This isn't just history; it's astronomy."

A surge of excitement coursed through me as the pieces of the puzzle began to click into place in my mind. The library, once merely a repository of knowledge, now revealed itself as a crucial waypoint on our journey—a guidepost pointing the way to our next clue. With each revelation, the anticipation of what lay ahead grew, igniting a spark of determination within me to unravel the mysteries that awaited us.

"The alignment...it must indicate a specific date," I suggested, my voice echoing off the ancient walls.

Dr. Bellamy pulled out her notebook and began sketching rapidly. "If we can calculate when these constellations were in this position relative to this location..."

"We'll have our date," Isaac finished.

Lila and I exchanged a glance, our spirits buoyed by the prospect of progress.

As Dr. Bellamy worked on the calculations, I paced along the wall, my fingers brushing over each carving as if I could absorb their stories through touch. The stone felt warm under my hand—warmer than it should have been—and I paused.

"Here," I called out, pressing against a section of the wall that seemed to emanate heat.

As the others gathered around me, their anticipation palpable in the air, I steeled myself for the task ahead. With every ounce of strength, I pushed against the unyielding stone, my fingers digging into its rough surface. With each exertion, I felt a subtle give, a faint hint of movement beneath my touch. And then, with a groan that seemed to echo through the ages, a section of the wall yielded, sliding back to reveal a passage hidden by ancient gears long dormant. The rush of adrenaline mixed with awe as we gazed into the darkness beyond, our path forward unveiled by our determination and teamwork.

"Rebecca!" Lila exclaimed with admiration clear in her tone.

Behind the wall was a narrow passageway leading down into darkness.

"We need light," Isaac said, pulling flashlights from his backpack.

We descended single file into the cool depths below. The passage twisted and turned until it opened into a small chamber lit by shafts of light from above. In its center stood an ornate pedestal carved from limestone, atop which lay an open book with pages so old they seemed ready to crumble at a touch.

"The Book of Harvests," Dr. Bellamy read aloud from an inscription on the pedestal.

Isaac approached cautiously, his light playing over pages filled with arcane symbols and cryptic notes.

"It looks like...instructions?" he mused.

Lila peered over his shoulder. "Instructions for what?"

I moved closer, examining each symbol and note as if they held keys to untold mysteries.

"It's for planting...and reaping." My eyes widened as understanding dawned on me. "But it's more than agriculture—it's symbolic."

Dr. Bellamy hummed thoughtfully. "What if 'planting' represents setting intentions and 'reaping' symbolizes achieving them? This could be metaphorical—a guide for success in any endeavor."

We pondered her words until Lila clapped her hands together with sudden clarity.

"That's it! We need to set our intentions—to find all pieces of the Austral Amulet—and this book is guiding us how!"

We looked at one another before Isaac stepped forward with resolve etched on his face.

"Let's do it then—let's set our intentions here and now."

We gathered around the book as one by one we voiced our deepest intentions—not just for finding pieces of an ancient artifact but for personal truths we sought on this journey: confidence for me, unity for Lila, trust for Isaac, and discovery for Dr. Bellamy.

Once we finished, we stood in silence—a bond forged deeper than before by shared hopes and dreams—until Lila gasped softly.

The book shimmered before us as if reacting to our collective wills, its pages flipping rapidly without any breeze to move them. They stopped abruptly on a page marked with an elaborate illustration of what appeared to be an underground cavern.

"There," I pointed at an X marked on part of the drawing where stalactites met stalagmites forming what resembled an altar or shrine within the cavern's depths.

Dr. Bellamy leaned forward excitedly. "That has to be where we'll find another piece of the Amulet!"

Our excitement grew tangible; success was within reach—a testament not just to our persistence but also my burgeoning leadership—a role I had never envisioned yet found myself embracing naturally under Eleanor's guiding influence even beyond her passing.

We copied down every detail from that page before carefully returning everything as we found it and retracing our steps back up into daylight carrying with us newfound determination and belief in ourselves and each other—a unity strengthened through trials faced together and victories hard-won against challenges that only history could devise.

The air was heavy with suspicion as Lila's gaze swept over us, one by one. We had been relying on her knowledge of the area, her easy familiarity with the locals, and the paths less trodden to navigate this labyrinthine city. Her assistance had been invaluable, but now, beneath the warm glow of a single lantern in a cramped room above a bustling market, trust was being put to the test.

"You've told me what you're after," Lila began, her arms folded across her chest. "But people don't just cross continents for old stories and family honor. What's really driving you? Why should I believe you're not just treasure hunters?"

Isaac shifted uncomfortably beside me. Dr. Bellamy adjusted her glasses, opening her mouth to speak, but I beat her to it.

"Lila," I said, my voice steady despite the flutter in my chest. "I understand your concern. It's hard to trust strangers who show up out of nowhere, claiming they're on some noble quest."

I reached into my bag and pulled out the tattered journal of Jeremiah Harley. "This isn't just about breaking some ancient curse or finding a piece of jewelry. It's about connecting with my past, understanding who I am. My great-grandmother believed in this—she believed in me."

Lila's eyes softened as she took in the sincerity in my voice, the way I held the journal like a sacred text.

Isaac chimed in, "Rebecca's not making this up. I've known her since we were kids. We used to dream about going on grand adventures together." He paused, his gaze finding mine with an intensity that left no room for doubt. "This is our chance to make a difference, not just for Rebecca's family but maybe for others too."

Dr. Bellamy nodded in agreement. "I wouldn't have left my research if I didn't think this was important, Lila. The Austral Amulet isn't just a trinket; it's a piece of history that could reshape our understanding of the past."

Lila sat down on an old wooden chair, the creaking sound punctuating the silence that followed our confessions. She studied each of us carefully as if weighing our words against some unseen scale.

"You three have something real between you," she said. "I can see that now." A smile flickered across her lips as she continued, "And I guess... I have my own reasons for helping you."

Our collective breath seemed to hang in the air as we waited for her to continue.

"My family has lived here for generations," Lila explained. "Legends say that part of the amulet was once hidden nearby, and that its power protected our people during hard times."

She stood up and walked over to a small window that looked out over the terracotta rooftops stretching into the night.

"Recently," she continued, turning back to face us with a determined look in her eyes, "things have been tough. If there's any truth to those stories... if there's any chance that finding this amulet could help... then I want to be part of it."

The tension that had built up moments before dissipated like mist under the morning sun. We had all come from different places and different lives, but we shared a common thread now—a bond woven through our intertwined fates and shared hopes.

We gathered closer around Lila as she spread out an old map on the table and pointed to a location where we might find our next clue.

"Together then," Dr. Bellamy declared.

"Together," we echoed in unison.

And so our alliance was sealed—not just as travelers on a shared journey but as companions who had found strength in each other's stories and resolve in each other's dreams.

Chapter 8

My breath came in short, sharp gasps as we edged along the narrow cliffside path. Isaac had his hand pressed firmly against the small of my back, a silent promise that he wouldn't let me fall. Dr. Bellamy led the way, her torchlight cutting through the dusk like a beacon of hope.

We had embarked on our quest for the second piece of the Austral Amulet what felt like eons ago, each clue plunging us further into perilous terrain. The ancient text we had painstakingly deciphered back in the city had foretold of its resting place being "guarded by stone and storm," but nothing could have adequately prepared us for the daunting reality that now lay before us. The very air seemed charged with anticipation as we stood at the threshold of our next trial, uncertainty mingling with determination in our hearts as we prepared to face whatever challenges lay ahead.

The winds howled around us, threatening to sweep us off our precarious trail. Below, waves crashed against jagged rocks, eager to claim anything—or anyone—that slipped. This piece was indeed proving harder to get, a test of our resolve and courage.

Finally, we reached a cave mouth that gaped like an open wound in the cliff face. Dr. Bellamy paused, her eyes scanning the darkened recess before us.

"This is it," she said with a certainty that sent shivers down my spine.

Delving deeper into the cave, we followed a subterranean river that wound from the heart of the cave to the sea. With no alternative path available, we braved the river despite its powerful flow challenging us. To prevent the current from dragging us back to the sea, we clasped hands and pressed on as one, the river's might opposing our advance, with only the enveloping darkness as our company. We battled the stream until, in the distance, we discerned a split leading to an open space. Stepping out of the water, Isaac seized his flashlight and cast its beam along the walls, revealing an array of enigmatic etchings.

While we scrutinised the carvings, Isaac meticulously arranged a few torch lights, projecting elongated silhouettes upon the rocky surfaces.

My heart raced as I traced my fingers over strange symbols etched into the stone—symbols that matched those in Jeremiah's journal.

The cave narrowed as we moved deeper, forcing us to squeeze through tight spaces and clamber over slippery rocks. The air grew colder, denser, filled with the weight of centuries passed in silence.

In a cavernous chamber deep within the cave, we found it: a pedestal carved from living rock stood proudly in the center. Atop it lay the second piece of the Austral Amulet, glowing faintly with an inner light that seemed to pulse in time with our quickened heartbeats.

Reaching out with trembling hands, I lifted the Amulet piece. It was heavier than I anticipated, its surface cool and smooth beneath my fingertips.

We had done it. Against all odds, we had found another piece of the Amulet.

Isaac, a bit winded, released a triumphant shout that reverberated against the stone while Dr. Bellamy offered a smile, her gaze filled with pride and a touch of worry.

"We've traveled a great distance," Isaac stated, regaining his breath. "Yet we mustn't forget that there are those who desire what we possess."

I nodded, suddenly aware of how vulnerable we were in this moment of victory. "Anton Kozlov is still out there," I added.

Dr. Bellamy sat down on a nearby boulder, her gaze distant. "Indeed," she said after a moment. "And with each piece we find, our journey grows more perilous."

We gathered close together then, our celebration muted by the gravity of what lay ahead. We were targets now; each success painted a brighter bullseye on our backs for those driven by greed and malice.

"But let's not forget why we're doing this," I said, gripping the Amulet piece tighter. "For family, for understanding... for breaking this curse."

Dr. Bellamy nodded solemnly and then cleared her throat as if preparing to shift gears mentally.

"Now," she began in her historian's tone that always commanded attention, "let's consider what this piece represents." She pointed to markings along its edge that I hadn't noticed before—delicate inscriptions forming an intricate pattern.

"These are ancient symbols of unity and protection," she explained. "The lore suggests that when combined with other pieces, it doesn't just break curses—it has the power to bind people together across differences."

Isaac whistled softly. "So it's not just about breaking a family curse," he mused aloud.

"No," Dr. Bellamy continued. "It's about bringing together those who have been torn apart—whether by fate or by their own doing."

Her words resonated within me; this quest was larger than any one person or any single family history—it was about connection on a grand scale.

I glanced at Isaac and saw my own wonder mirrored in his eyes. The Amulet wasn't just an artifact; it was a symbol of hope for unity amidst division—a timely reminder in our fractured world.

Dr. Bellamy gestured toward the chamber walls where scenes were carved into the rock: people from different walks of life coming together around an object that glowed like a star—a representation of the Amulet itself.

"These carvings... they tell a story older than any of us can fathom," she whispered.

As I stood flanked by my two companions, their faces aglow in the warm light of our lanterns, I was overcome by a profound sense of purpose. In that moment, I realized that this journey was no longer just mine to bear; it belonged to all who dared to dream of a world made whole once more. Together, we stood on the threshold of something greater than ourselves, united by a shared vision and a boundless determination to see it through to fruition.

With newfound respect for our mission and its ancient roots, we packed away our gear and prepared to leave this hallowed place behind—for now—with another precious piece secured and another step closer to fulfilling Jeremiah Harley's legacy and perhaps something even greater than any of us had imagined.

Anton Kozlov stood sentinel upon the ridge, a solitary figure silhouetted against the canvas of the bleeding horizon, where crimson and gold hues melded in a twilight embrace. His gaze, sharp as a falcon's, swept over the landscape below with a predatory intensity, every contour of the land mapped out in his mind's eye. Lines etched deep into his weathered face bore witness to a lifetime of pursuit and determination.

Here, in this desolate expanse where time and neglect had buried history beneath layers of earth, Anton had tracked them—the seekers of the ancient relic. He understood the value of what Rebecca and her companions sought; it pulsed through his veins like a primal hunger, a thirst for power that mirrored his own insatiable ambition.

He had always been a man of considerable means, his wealth amassed through the acquisition of rare artifacts and the ruthless pursuit of treasures untold. Yet, it was not wealth alone that fueled Anton's relentless pursuit. It was the promise of control, the potential to shape destiny itself with the Astral Amulet's might. And he would stop at nothing to claim it.

As the sun dipped below the horizon, Anton descended from his vantage point and strode toward a waiting vehicle, a sleek black SUV that blended into the shadows of dusk. Inside, a team of operatives sprang to life at his approach. They were a handpicked crew—experts in logistics, surveillance, and acquisition.

One operative, a woman with sharp eyes and an even sharper mind, handed Anton a tablet displaying a map peppered with red dots. "They've made progress," she said, her voice as cold as steel. "But we're closing in."

Anton traced a finger over the glowing screen, following the breadcrumb trail left by Rebecca's group. "They are clever," he mused aloud. "But not clever enough to evade my network."

His network was extensive—a web of informants and contacts that spanned continents. Antique dealers whispered rumors into his ear; corrupt officials bent to his will; even the fringes of academia were not immune to his influence. It was through these channels that Anton learned of Dr. Bellamy's expertise and Rebecca's inheritance—the diary that held secrets others could only dream of deciphering.

"Sir," another operative chimed in, "we've tapped into local communications. There's talk among the villagers about foreigners searching for relics." The operative paused before adding with a smirk, "It seems they've made quite an impression."

"Good," Anton replied. "Keep listening. I want updates on their every move."

He didn't just want updates; he demanded them—commanding his resources with an iron grip that left no room for failure. The stakes were too high, and Anton had invested too much to let this opportunity slip through his fingers.

The night grew deeper as Anton and his team mobilized once more, their vehicles slicing through darkness like specters haunting the roads less traveled. Each member knew their role—tracking devices planted, satellite imagery scoured for heat signatures, coded messages bouncing across secure lines—all in service to one man's ambition.

As dawn approached, Anton stood before another overlook, gazing upon an ancient structure where he suspected they would soon arrive—the next waypoint on their journey marked by Jeremiah Harley's cryptic clues.

"Sir," an operative reported breathlessly as he approached him from behind. "We have confirmation—they're heading towards the old monastery."

A thin smile crept across Anton's lips; they were playing right into his hands.

"Prepare for our arrival," he instructed without turning to face him. "And ensure our local assets are ready."

The group remained oblivious to the encroaching danger as they delved deeper into their quest—the pieces of the amulet beckoning them onward like shards of starlight calling out to kindred spirits lost in night's embrace.

Rebecca clutched the diary close as they gathered their belongings and readied themselves for what lay ahead—a test of wills against time itself and those who sought to rewrite its course.

"We need to be cautious," Dr. Bellamy warned as they packed their gear into weathered backpacks.

Isaac nodded in agreement, double-checking their supplies before glancing up at Rebecca with a reassuring smile that belied his own concerns. "We've got this," he said confidently.

They had no way of knowing that each step forward tightened the noose around their necks—that every clue deciphered brought them closer not only to their goal but also to a man whose hunger for power mirrored the darkness before dawn.

As they set out from their makeshift campsite, they failed to notice a figure watching from afar—a silent sentinel biding its time until action became necessary.

Anton Kozlov retreated into shadow once more as Rebecca's group moved on—three souls bound by fate and flanked by unseen forces eager to claim victory in a race against time itself.

The day passed with tense anticipation as Anton monitored their progress—a game of cat and mouse played on a board stretching across history's canvas. He respected Rebecca's tenacity but saw her only as an obstacle between him and what was rightfully his by virtue of ambition alone.

Night fell once again—a cloak draped over a world holding its breath in wait for what was to come. As Rebecca and her companions settled down for rest beneath stars that bore silent witness to their plight, Anton prepared for what he knew would be an inevitable confrontation—a meeting between those who held keys to untold power in their grasp.

And so ended another chapter in their tale—one fraught with danger lurking just beyond perception's edge—an edge Anton Kozlov teetered upon with intent as sharp as a knife's blade poised above heart's beat racing toward destiny unknown.

⸺ • ◉ • ⸺

The cool morning air wrapped around us like a gentle shroud as we prepared to leave. Isaac was double-checking our packs, ensuring the latest piece of the Austral Amulet was nestled securely among our belongings. Dr. Bellamy, with a careful hand, wrapped the fragment in a soft cloth, placing it in a hard case designed to withstand the rigors of travel. The piece itself, no larger than a child's fist, seemed to pulse with an energy that belied its size. I could feel its warmth through the fabric as if it sought to reassure me of its presence.

We moved methodically, each of us lost in our tasks. Isaac's fingers worked with the precision of a craftsman, his blue eyes focused intently on every buckle and strap. Dr. Bellamy scribbled last-minute notes in her journal, her brows furrowed in concentration. And I... I paused.

For a moment, I allowed myself to reflect on the progress we had made—the journey from my small bedroom, filled with longing and quiet desperation, to this vast expanse of history and discovery. I traced the path we had taken on the map with my finger, each location a testament to our resilience.

I thought of Eleanor and Jeremiah Harley and the legacy they left behind—a legacy that now rested partly in my hands. The realization was humbling and empowering all at once. My great-grandmother's pendant lay against my chest, a constant companion whispering courage into my heart.

In this moment of solitude, amid the clinking gear and rustling maps, I realized how much I had changed. The girl who once sought invisibility now pursued visibility in the most extraordinary way possible. Purpose coursed through me with every beat of my heart, aligning with the rhythm of our quest.

A gentle hand on my shoulder brought me back from my reverie. Lila stood beside me, her curly black hair catching glints of sunlight, her bright smile a beacon in the early dawn.

"It's time," she said.

I nodded and turned to face her fully. She held out her hand; within it lay a small cross pendant on a delicate chain.

"For protection," Lila murmured as she draped it over my head. The cross settled near Eleanor's pendant—a tangible symbol of the trust and alliances we had forged on this journey.

"Thank you," I whispered, my fingers closing tightly around both pendants as if they were lifelines in a sea of uncertainty. In their weight, I found solace and strength, grounding me amidst the tumultuous currents of our journey.

Lila embraced me then—a fierce hug that spoke volumes about her kind-hearted nature. "Remember," she said as she pulled back just enough to look into my eyes, "you're never alone."

Her words echoed within me as we exchanged farewells. Isaac clapped Lila on the back with an easy camaraderie that spoke of battles faced together. Dr. Bellamy thanked Lila for her invaluable assistance with a sincerity that resonated deeply.

We shouldered our packs and turned toward our next destination—the unknown stretching before us like an uncharted melody waiting to be played. Lila's token joined the symphony of artifacts we carried: a chorus of history, faith, and friendship harmonizing to guide us forward.

As we stepped away from that place where history had whispered its secrets through stone and dust, I realized that this journey was not just about finding pieces of an amulet or lifting ancient curses—it was about discovering pieces of ourselves and lifting each other up when we faltered.

With one last glance back at Lila waving goodbye from afar, I turned toward what awaited us next—my heart steady, my resolve unwavering.

Chapter 9

I remember the sinking feeling in my stomach, like I was falling through clouds of uncertainty. The van we were in, an old, rickety thing with peeling paint and a driver who claimed he knew every shortcut in the country, rattled down the dusty road. It was supposed to be a shortcut to our next location. Instead, it had become a roadblock in our journey. A loud pop echoed through the air as the vehicle lurched to one side.

"Flat tire," Isaac muttered, confirming my fears. He pushed his way out of the van before it had even come to a complete stop.

I followed suit, stepping out into the blistering heat that enveloped me like a suffocating blanket. The dusty road kicked up a fine film, coating my throat as I watched Isaac with an exasperated sigh, his brow furrowed in frustration as he examined the tyre.

"This is just great," he said, his voice laced with sarcasm. "Because we really needed more delays."

Dr. Bellamy stepped out behind us, her eyes scanning our surroundings before settling on the deflated tire. "It's not ideal, but it's fixable," she offered with calm reassurance.

The driver shrugged apologetically, explaining that he didn't carry a spare – something about it being stolen last month and him not having the money to replace it yet.

Isaac kicked at the dirt, frustration radiating off him like waves of heat from the pavement. "We can't afford to lose any more time," he said through gritted teeth.

Tension crackled in the air as his words hung between us, heavy with accusation. Annoyance surged within me, propelled by the weight of our predicament. "We wouldn't be losing time if you hadn't insisted on this 'reliable' guide," I retorted, unable to contain the frustration that simmered beneath the surface.

His blue eyes flashed toward me. "You think this is my fault?"

"Well, you were so sure of yourself when you hired him!" My voice rose higher than I intended.

The tension between us was palpable; our words were daggers disguised as whispers. We stood there under the relentless sun, two friends divided by unforeseen circumstances and mounting pressure.

Dr. Bellamy intervened before we could go any further down this heated path. "Let's not turn on each other," she said. "These things happen."

She approached the driver and spoke in hushed tones while Isaac and I avoided each other's gaze. Moments later, she returned with a plan.

"There's a village not too far from here," Dr. Bellamy announced. "The driver knows someone who might have a spare tire or can at least help us get to town."

Isaac nodded reluctantly, and I could see him mentally recalibrating our plans.

"Let's grab what we need and head that way," Dr. Bellamy continued. "It'll be faster on foot."

As we trudged through the unforgiving terrain toward hope of salvation for our travel woes, I could feel Isaac's irritation simmering alongside my own guilt for snapping at him earlier.

We trudged onward in silence, the weight of our shared burdens hanging heavy in the air, until Dr. Bellamy finally spoke, her voice cutting through the quiet like a beacon in the darkness. "This journey is testing us all," she remarked, her gaze moving between us with a blend of kindness and determination that mirrored Eleanor's when she imparted crucial lessons.

Isaac exhaled sharply before turning to me with an expression that was part frustration, part apology. "I'm sorry for earlier," he admitted. "I'm just... worried about everything."

My shoulders slumped slightly as I met his gaze. "Me too," I confessed, my voice softer now.

The weight of our mission pressed down on us – finding the Austral Amulet wasn't just about adventure; it was about family legacy and breaking curses.

Dr. Bellamy kept pace beside us as peacekeeper and guide in more ways than one – leading us through rocky paths both literal and metaphorical.

We continued onward, our resolve hardening with each step taken together under her watchful eye.

<hr />

We had finally made it. Our boots clung to the earth with a layer of dust, marking our passage through arid lands and over rocky outcrops. The village lay nestled in a valley, a cluster of buildings hugging the curve of a lazy river that snaked through like a lifeline. Isaac, Dr. Bellamy, and I stood at the edge, overlooking the culmination of miles travelled and challenges faced.

"This... is more than just distance covered," I said, my voice trailing off as I absorbed the sight. "It's every doubt we've overcome."

Isaac wiped his brow, a smile playing on his lips. "And every wrong turn that turned out right."

Dr. Bellamy adjusted her glasses, peering down at the village with a thoughtful gaze. "And it's only a part of what we're set to achieve."

We descended into the heart of the village just as dusk began to weave its cool fingers through the warmth of day. Locals regarded us with cautious curiosity, their eyes following our weary trio as we found a suitable spot to rest for the night just beyond the outskirts.

The campfire crackled to life, its glow casting dancing shadows on our faces as night descended like a velvet curtain. We gathered around the warmth, each lost in thought until the silence begged to be filled.

Isaac broke it first. "I never thought I'd be part of something like this." He prodded the fire with a stick, sending sparks spiraling into the sky. "I was ready for life to be... simple. Predictable."

Dr. Bellamy chuckled softly. "Life has an interesting way of steering us off course." She added another log to the fire, her face illuminated by the flame's embrace.

"I was afraid," I confessed, my voice barely above a whisper. "Afraid of being invisible forever, unseen by everyone... even myself."

Isaac turned towards me, his expression softening. "You've never been invisible to me, Bec."

A silence settled over us once more, not uncomfortable but filled with unspoken understanding.

"It's funny," Dr. Bellamy mused after a moment, her eyes reflecting the firelight. "The things we fear often lead us to discover strengths we never knew we had."

We nodded in agreement, each pondering her words and finding our own truths within them.

"And what about you?" Isaac asked Dr. Bellamy after some time had passed.

She sighed, poking at the embers with a thoughtful air. "My fear is history forgotten—stories lost to time without anyone to tell them." She paused before continuing with a hint of vulnerability in her voice. "And my hope... is that we're making history right now."

"That we are," Isaac said with conviction.

A lull in conversation gave way to contemplation as we each tended to our personal thoughts and fears like one tends embers in a dying fire—gently coaxing them into something that could give warmth and light.

After several moments of quiet reflection, Dr. Bellamy leaned forward slightly as if she held a secret at the tip of her tongue.

"You know," she began in an almost conspiratorial tone, "there's an old legend about amulets such as ours." We leaned in closer; even amidst our weariness, curiosity remained ever-potent.

"They say these amulets were not just mere trinkets but repositories of collective will—the desires and hopes of those who crafted them." Her eyes glinted with scholarly passion as she spoke.

Isaac raised an eyebrow but remained silent, while I listened intently.

"The power they held wasn't just mystical—it was symbolic too," she continued. "Binding people together across generations through shared beliefs and common purpose."

Her words wove through my mind like threads pulling together pieces of an ancient tapestry.

"However," Dr. Bellamy added after a pause that seemed to draw out longer than it actually was, "Jeremiah's journal contained a stark warning about such artifacts." She reached into her bag and pulled out the weathered journal we'd become so familiar with on our journey.

"Only those who are blood descendants can truly possess it," she read aloud from Jeremiah's scrawling handwriting that spread across one yellowed page.

Isaac's gaze bore into me, intense and unyielding, sending a shiver down my spine. I swallowed hard, a knot forming in my throat, as I tried to decipher the unspoken message behind his eyes.

"Anyone else who dares claim it invites misfortune upon themselves and their lineage," Dr. Bellamy finished with gravity tinging her voice.

The fire popped loudly as if punctuating her statement—a sound that seemed louder than usual in the quiet that followed her revelation.

Isaac let out a long breath he seemed unaware he'd been holding. "So it really is up to you then, Rebecca."

My hands instinctively reached for my great-grandmother's pendant resting against my chest—a tangible connection to my lineage and now this amulet that seemed more burdensome yet more vital than ever before.

"I... I understand what needs to be done," I replied.

Dr. Bellamy closed Jeremiah's journal gently and placed it back into her bag before offering me an encouraging smile—a silent pledge of support that spoke louder than any words could have in that moment.

The fire continued its dance as we sat around it—three individuals bound by fate and choice on this improbable quest; three individuals who had grown closer through shared hardships and hopes; three individuals facing an uncertain future armed only with each other and an unyielding resolve to see this journey through no matter what lay ahead.

—— • ◦ ◉ ◦ • ——

The van rumbled into the heart of the unassuming town just as the sun dipped below the horizon, painting the sky with strokes of pink and orange. Isaac, Dr. Bellamy, and I had grown accustomed to each other's company over the course of our journey, but a new tire on the guide's old van offered a fresh sense of progress.

We disembarked in a quaint square lined with cobblestone streets and aging buildings that whispered stories of yesteryears. As we stretched our legs, a woman approached us, her presence like a gentle breeze on a stifling day.

"Hello there! You folks look like you're far from home," she said, her voice a melody that seemed to resonate with an inexplicable familiarity.

"I'm Penelope Lenz," she continued, extending a hand that carried the warmth of home.

"Rebecca Harley," I responded, clasping Penelope's hand firmly and feeling an instant connection, as if Eleanor herself had orchestrated this encounter from beyond the veil. Isaac and Dr. Bellamy followed suit, introducing themselves with nods of acknowledgment, each exchanging pleasantries with our newfound acquaintance.

Penelope's eyes lingered on my great-grandmother's pendant that always hung around my neck. A smile danced on her lips as if she recognized it from a dream or a distant memory.

"You're here for the Amulet, aren't you?" she asked, not as a question but as an affirmation.

Dr. Bellamy raised an eyebrow in intrigue while Isaac glanced at me with caution. How did she know? The thought circled my mind like an eagle riding the thermals.

"We are," I said after a moment's hesitation. "But how could you possibly know that?"

Penelope chuckled softly. "This town may not look like much, but it's full of secrets and whispers of the past. The Austral Amulet is one such whisper."

She invited us to her home, a cozy abode filled with antiques and artifacts that could have belonged in Dr. Bellamy's museum. As we sat down in her living room surrounded by history, Penelope served us tea and began to unravel tales of the Amulet's lore.

"It's said that long ago, an ancient society held control over the pieces of the Amulet," Penelope explained, her voice painting images in our minds. "They knew its power to unite people wasn't just metaphorical—it was real magic."

Dr. Bellamy leaned forward, captivated by every word as she scribbled notes into her already overflowing journal.

"The Amulet pieces were scattered by design," Penelope continued, "to bring together those who were meant to find them."

I felt Eleanor's stories intertwining with Penelope's words—like melodies harmonizing in an intricate song—and it gave me strength.

Penelope rose from her seat and walked over to a bookshelf laden with leather-bound volumes and delicate trinkets. She withdrew an old map, its edges frayed with time.

"This map leads to an important site for your quest," she said, laying it out on the coffee table before us.

Isaac studied it closely, his fingers tracing routes and landmarks while Dr. Bellamy cross-referenced it with Jeremiah's journal entries.

"The path is treacherous," Penelope warned. "But I believe you three have been chosen for this journey."

Her words hung in the air, heavy with a sense of inevitability, enveloping us like a cloak of fate being woven anew. It was a feeling at once exhilarating and daunting, as if the weight of destiny itself rested upon our shoulders, urging us forward into the unknown with both trepidation and resolve.

With renewed determination, we thanked Penelope for her kindness and wisdom. She was more than just a guide; she was a reminder of Eleanor and Jeremiah—their spirit seemed to live within her.

Before we retired for the evening, Penelope presented me with a diminutive compass, its surface etched with elaborate designs—a further slice of antiquity to assist us on our voyage.

"Keep this close," she said. "It'll serve you well when times get tough."

<hr />

I awoke to the sound of the bustling town Penelope called home. The air carried a cacophony of voices, each with its own timbre and rhythm, weaving a tapestry of life that hummed with diversity. I watched from the window as people of different backgrounds and cultures moved through the streets below, a fluid dance of cooperation and mutual respect.

Isaac stood beside me, his gaze following the ebb and flow of the crowd. "It's something else, isn't it?" he murmured, his voice laced with wonder. "Everyone's so different, yet they're all part of the same picture."

Dr. Bellamy joined us, adjusting her glasses as she peered out. "It's a reminder," she began, "that history isn't just about artifacts and old texts. It's about people—how they come together, how they learn from each other."

As we ventured out into the morning light, I felt a sense of unity that transcended language and appearance. Shopkeepers greeted customers in multiple languages, children played games that melded cultural traditions, and food stalls offered a fusion of flavours that spoke to the town's collective heritage.

At one stall, Isaac reached for a piece of fruit unfamiliar to him. The vendor, noticing Isaac's hesitation, smiled warmly and explained its origin and taste. Isaac listened intently, nodding in appreciation as he sampled the exotic flavour.

"Never thought I'd like something I couldn't even pronounce," he confessed with a grin.

I laughed along with him but realized that my own biases had been gently challenged. Here was a place where differences weren't just tolerated; they were celebrated.

We followed Penelope through the heart of town toward a small park where people gathered to share stories. She gestured toward an elderly man recounting tales to an audience of captivated children.

"Empathy," Penelope said as we drew near enough to listen. "It's what binds us all together. When we truly understand another's feelings and experiences, we bridge gaps wider than oceans."

Her words struck a chord deep within me, resonating with my own experiences. How many times had I yearned for someone who truly understood me? Eleanor had been that person once—a beacon of understanding and solace in a world that often felt vast and indifferent.

As Penelope spoke of empathy, her face illuminated with an inner fire, radiant with passion and sincerity. Her words resonated deeply within me, echoing my own journey of self-discovery and the newfound confidence I had begun to cultivate in my empathetic nature. In that moment, it felt as though our paths had converged for a reason, intertwining in a shared quest for understanding and compassion.

A young girl approached us hesitantly, clutching a worn-out doll. Her eyes flitted between our faces before settling on mine. In them, I saw a reflection of my younger self—searching for connection.

I knelt down to her level and smiled encouragingly. "She's lovely," I said, gesturing to the doll. "What's her name?"

The girl beamed, her shyness melting away as she launched into a story about her doll's adventures—stories not unlike those Eleanor used to share with me.

In that moment, it became clear how empathy could bridge worlds. Through understanding her perspective, I connected with the girl in a way that felt almost magical—a shared moment across different lives.

Isaac observed us with a gentle expression, his features softening with understanding. In that moment, it seemed as though he grasped the deeper significance of our mission—it wasn't solely about unearthing an ancient artifact, but about forging meaningful connections with others on a profound level. It was about empathy, understanding, and the bonds that transcended time and circumstance.

Penelope's words continued to weave their spell around us as she shared anecdotes of her own travels—moments where empathy had opened doors and mended fences.

"It's easy to get caught up in our own views," Dr. Bellamy mused aloud after listening to one such tale. "But when we step into someone else's shoes—even for just a moment—it changes everything."

The day unfolded like a lesson in humanity: Each interaction chipped away at our preconceived notions and replaced them with understanding and connection.

As evening approached, Penelope led us back to her modest home where we gathered around the kitchen table laden with dishes from different corners of the world—a visual representation of the day's lessons.

Over dinner, Penelope shared more about herself—how her grandmother had influenced her thinking and how she strived to live by those teachings.

Rebecca Harley listened intently as Penelope Lenz spoke across the dinner table lit by flickering candles casting warm shadows on the walls around us—a comforting contrast to the chill evening air seeping through an open window somewhere behind me.

Penelope's voice was soft yet carried weight; it was filled with stories inherited from generations past yet grounded in present truths that demanded attention in their simplicity.

"Empathy is more than understanding others; it's seeing their joys as your joys and their sorrows as your sorrows," Penelope explained as she passed around steaming plates of food that smelled like different corners of the earth combined into one kitchen.

Her words resonated with a truth I had long understood but hadn't always put into practice: true understanding went beyond mere listening—it required the ability to empathize, to truly feel what others felt without losing sight of one's own identity in the process. It was a delicate balance, a skill honed through experience and a willingness to open oneself to the emotions of others while maintaining a firm grounding in one's own sense of self.

I glanced at Isaac who sat opposite me; his eyes reflected the flickering candlelight while he absorbed Penelope's message with a thoughtful expression etched across his face—a silent admission that perhaps there were depths within himself yet unexplored or understood by others.

Dr. Bellamy nodded along from beside him, her face illuminated by both candlelight and revelation—the kind only true listening can bring forth when we allow ourselves to hear beyond words spoken out loud into silent spaces between them where true meanings reside waiting for discovery.

A comfortable silence settled over us as we ate; it was as if Penelope's home became our refuge from chaos outside—a place where barriers fell away leaving only human connections in their purest form allowing for growth beyond personal misconceptions towards collective understanding within this diverse group brought together by fate or destiny depending on one's belief system which seemed less important than reality before us here now together on this journey not just towards finding Austral Amulet but also towards finding pieces within ourselves long lost or forgotten until now revealed under watchful eyes caring hearts around this table tonight under stars hidden behind clouds overhead whispering winds carrying our shared stories far wide reaching corners unknown even unto ourselves until this moment right here right now forever imprinted within memories carried forward into tomorrow's unknown adventures waiting just beyond horizon's edge calling us forth beckoning come explore come learn come grow come be more than you ever thought possible before because this is what life is all about really isn't it?

Penelope's home felt like a patch of sunlight in a dense forest, warm and inviting. Her walls, adorned with maps and old photographs, told stories of countless adventures. As she laid out a series of cryptic notes and weathered pages before us, I could see Isaac and Dr. Bellamy leaning in, their curiosity piqued.

"These," Penelope said, pointing to the documents with a slender finger, "are my great-grandfather's notes that he compiled on the Amulet. He was as much an adventurer as your Jeremiah Harley."

I brushed my fingers over the yellowed papers, feeling the weight of history in every word. It was as if Eleanor and Jeremiah had led us to Penelope, another piece in this sprawling puzzle stretching across generations.

"The third piece," Penelope continued, her voice tinged with excitement, "is said to lie within the heart of an ancient forest. The locals speak of a tree that stands out from the rest – older, wiser, and more alive. They call it 'The Sentinel.'"

Dr. Bellamy adjusted her glasses, scrutinizing the notes. "The tree could be a marker," she mused.

Isaac folded his arms, looking thoughtfully at the papers. "So we're looking for one particular tree in an entire forest? That's finding a needle in a haystack."

I felt a spark within me as I surveyed the room. The pendant around my neck seemed to pulse with warmth, emboldening me.

"No," I said, my voice steadier than I felt. "It's not just any tree; it's The Sentinel. We have legends back home about trees that watch over entire forests. If this tree is as important as Penelope says, there will be signs leading to it – paths used by those who revered it."

Penelope nodded approvingly. "Exactly. My great-grandfather wrote about natural markers – rock formations, streams that form patterns – all leading to The Sentinel."

I reached for the notes and spread them out like a fan. Each one held clues: sketches of leaves, peculiarly twisted branches, all forming a breadcrumb trail to follow.

"Look here," I pointed out to Isaac and Dr. Bellamy. "These drawings... they're not random trees; they're signposts." My finger traced the path laid out by the sketches.

Isaac leaned over my shoulder, his presence comforting despite our past tensions. "You're onto something, Rebecca," he admitted with a grin.

Dr. Bellamy peered at the sketches with professional interest. "This one here," she indicated a drawing of a branch twisted into an almost deliberate shape, "seems particularly intentional."

"Then that's where we start," I decided.

Penelope clapped her hands together softly. "Brilliant! You have your great-grandmother's intuition and your great-great-grandfather's spirit."

We spent hours poring over the maps and notes until we could recite every clue from memory.

As dawn crept into Penelope's cozy study, casting long shadows across our huddled group, we knew it was time to move on.

"We've got all we need." Isaac stood up first, stretching his arms above his head.

Dr. Bellamy closed one of the heavy books with a soft thud and nodded in agreement.

I took one last look at Penelope who gave me an encouraging smile. "Go on," she said, her eyes sparkling with unspoken stories.

The three of us made our way outside where the early morning light painted everything gold. It was another beginning; the clues from Penelope had breathed new life into our search.

When our guide fired up the engine of the aged vehicle – which appeared more battered than when we initially journeyed in it yet remained dependable – a wave of resolve energized me.

We were no longer just wanderers; we were seekers with purpose and direction.

"Next stop: The Sentinel," I declared with newfound confidence.

Dr. Bellamy offered a nod of approval as Isaac's grin accompanied our departure onto the path that would draw us into the thick folds of fate.

With each mile that rolled beneath us, it felt like pieces of an elaborate tapestry were falling into place – both within our quest for the Amulet and within ourselves.

Chapter 10

U nder the cloak of dusk, Anton Kozlov perched on the hood of his now weathered vehicle, a relic from his earlier expeditions. He flicked through the images on his phone with a hunter's precision, each one a snapshot of Rebecca, Isaac, and Dr. Bellamy. His source had been diligent, documenting every turn and detour the trio made.

"Smart kids," Anton muttered to himself. His eyes, dark pools reflecting the dying light, scanned the horizon where he last saw them vanish. He knew they were close—his instincts never failed him.

He was not alone in his quest; beside him, his satellite phone buzzed relentlessly. Messages poured in, a steady stream of updates from contacts scattered like breadcrumbs along the protagonists' path. A local innkeeper remembered the young adventurers' curious questions. A gas station attendant recounted the peculiar group that stopped for fuel and supplies.

Anton traced their route on a map spread across the vehicle's bonnet. They had taken a detour through an old village, a decision that baffled him momentarily until he saw the pattern—the path less traveled, less conspicuous. It was clever, but not enough to elude him.

With night fully upon him, Anton slipped into his vehicle, its engine growling to life at his command. He drove through the labyrinth of back roads and forgotten trails as if he were drawing them from memory. Each twist and turn brought him closer to his quarry.

He stopped for nothing and no one, save for brief exchanges with locals who could be persuaded to part with information for the right price. Anton's charm was as much a tool as any gadget in his arsenal.

In an abandoned farmhouse that served as a makeshift command center, Anton's fingers danced over maps littered with notes and photos pinned alongside strings that formed a web of pursuit. Each piece connected to another—a web of strategy woven with care.

The room echoed with silence save for the scratch of pen on paper as he marked another potential intercept point. "Patience," he whispered to himself, "the game is just beginning."

The chill of anticipation settled over him like a second skin as he considered his next move. He had resources—people who owed him favors and others who feared him enough to do his bidding without question.

A smirk played on Anton's lips; it was only a matter of time before he would make his move and claim what he deemed rightfully his—the Astral Amulet and its untold powers.

In that quiet room where shadows clung to every corner, Anton sat back in an old chair that creaked under his weight. The light from a single bulb cast an eerie glow across his sharp features as he contemplated the chase ahead.

The trio believed they were outsmarting their unknown pursuer by taking detours and using disguises, but they were merely pawns in Anton's grand strategy—a game of chess where he was always two moves ahead.

He savored this part of the hunt—the calculation, the anticipation before closing in on his prey. With each step Rebecca and her group took toward uncovering the Amulet's secrets, they unknowingly led Anton closer to victory.

He could almost feel the weight of the Amulet in his hands; it called to him through history and legend—a siren song promising power and control beyond mortal comprehension.

As midnight approached, Anton Kozlov stood up and extinguished the light, plunging the room into darkness once more. Outside, an owl hooted its nightly serenade while somewhere distant yet drawing nearer by each passing moment were Rebecca, Isaac, and Dr. Bellamy—oblivious to how tightly they were woven into Anton's tapestry of deceit.

And so ended another day in their perilous journey—a day that brought them one step closer to their destiny and one step closer to Anton Kozlov's trap.

The van's tires crunched over the gravel as we wound our way through a landscape that felt more ancient than time itself. Trees clawed at the sky, their dense canopy blotting out the sun and casting us in perpetual twilight. Our travel guides grip on the steering wheel tightened, knuckles pale against the leather. Dr. Bellamy sat beside him, maps spread across her lap, tracing our path with a delicate finger.

Once more, I found myself unable to shake the unsettling sensation of being watched. Whether it was the eerie silence of the forest or the way shadows seemed to dance and slither between the trees, an unexplained chill crawled up my spine, sending shivers down my arms. Despite the stuffiness of the van, I couldn't help but rub my arms for warmth, seeking solace in the physical contact as I cast wary glances into the darkness beyond.

"This terrain is unforgiving," Dr. Bellamy murmured, her voice barely above the hum of the engine. "Legends speak of spirits that guard these woods, punishing those who disrespect their domain."

Isaac gave a derisive snort. "Just old wives' tales," he muttered, yet his gaze darted anxiously toward the back glass.

I leaned forward between them. "What kind of spirits?" My voice was a whisper, reverence for this place and its lore instinctive.

"Protectors of ancient artefacts," she replied. "They say when you hear the wind howl against the rocks, it's them warning off intruders."

A gust rattled through the trees just then, as if on cue, and Isaac's snort turned into a swallow. The road—or what passed for one—narrowed further, and branches scraped against the van like fingernails on metal.

"Careful," I cautioned as our guide navigated around a particularly menacing boulder that loomed at the edge of our path.

"I see it," he shot back, concentration etched into his brow.

A strained hush enveloped us, with Isaac scrutinizing the driver's every move and Dr. Bellamy intermittently suggesting which way to go. I remained vigilant, searching for any clues that would align with the details in Jeremiah's diary or the extensive understanding Dr. Bellamy possessed.

It wasn't long before we encountered our first real obstacle: a fallen tree blocking our way forward. Our guide brought us to a shuddering halt mere inches from its thick trunk.

"Looks like we're on foot from here," Isaac said.

Dr. Bellamy and I exchanged glances before nodding in agreement. We couldn't let a tree stop us—not when we were so close to another piece of the Amulet.

Exiting the van, we surveyed our surroundings warily. The forest seemed to close in around us as we worked together to move branches and smaller debris out of our path.

"Remember," Dr. Bellamy said as we heaved against larger limbs, "respect is key."

In a solemn pact of unspoken understanding, we worked in silence, mindful not to disrupt the tranquility any further than our presence already had. With each careful movement of a branch, it felt as though we were piecing together a delicate agreement with whatever unseen entities observed us from within the depths of the forest. The air hung heavy with anticipation, as if the very trees themselves held their breath, awaiting the outcome of our silent negotiation.

After clearing enough space for us to pass through, we returned to the van only to find it wouldn't start again—its engine groaning in protest before falling silent once more.

"We'll have to continue on foot," Isaac decided after their driver made several failed attempts to revive it.

Dr. Bellamy nodded her assent while I fetched our backpacks from the backseat. Our journey was about to become much more arduous without wheels beneath us.

As if sensing our predicament, an owl hooted ominously from somewhere deep within the forest—a sound so mournful it seemed like an echo from another world.

"That's not just any owl," Dr. Bellamy whispered as we shouldered our packs and locked up the useless van behind us.

"The locals believe it's a sign," she continued as we began our trek into denser underbrush, "a portent of trials ahead."

I could feel Isaac's unease without looking at him; it vibrated off him like heat from pavement on a summer day. We pushed deeper into the forest's heart with every step and I wondered if this was how Jeremiah had felt all those years ago—driven by purpose but haunted by omens and warnings whispered on winds and carried by creatures of flight.

The further we went, the more tangible those warnings became; carvings on tree trunks that weren't just scars of nature but symbols meant to ward off—or perhaps lure in—the unwary traveller.

"What do they mean?" I asked when one such carving—a spiral with eyes etched at its centre—seemed to follow us with its gaze.

"They're old markers," Dr. Bellamy explained without breaking stride. "They say these symbols are meant to protect sacred places."

"And are we... trespassing?" My voice hitched with concern.

Dr. Bellamy paused then, turning her sharp eyes upon me in consideration before answering slowly, "We're seeking understanding—not exploitation."

The conviction in her voice steadied me more than I'd care to admit aloud. If Dr. Bellamy believed in our quest's integrity, then who was I to doubt?

Our path became rougher still; roots twisted like serpents underfoot while vines hung low enough to catch in our hair if we weren't careful enough to duck or weave around them.

Isaac helped me over a particularly large root that tripped me up despite my vigilance—a small act but one that spoke volumes about how much we'd come to rely on each other out here where civilization seemed a distant memory.

And then there were whispers—not words exactly but sighs carried by breezes that sent shivers down my spine despite their subtlety—a language of this place that none of us could speak but all of us understood on some primal level: caution tread lightly you are not alone here.

Our collective breaths fogged in front of us as dusk approached sooner beneath these ancient boughs than it would have out in open air—and with nightfall came new sounds; creatures that called this place home beginning their nocturnal routines while those diurnal sought shelter and rest until light returned—if it ever truly did within these woods' embrace...

We huddled close without speaking it aloud—our pact sealed tighter with every shared glance every brush of shoulder against shoulder—companions bound by circumstance and something deeper still; something forged by firelight and stars whispered secrets shared burdens... And through it all hung heavy that sense of foreboding—an anticipation not entirely unpleasant but unnerving nonetheless; like waiting for thunder after lightning has already flashed too close for comfort...

Thick foliage encased us as we trudged through the underbrush, the map in my hand growing damp with sweat. The travel guides old van, abandoned miles back on a semblance of a road, seemed like a distant memory now. I couldn't shake the feeling that we were going in circles, that every tree and rock was taunting us with its familiarity.

"We've passed that same gnarled tree twice now," Isaac grumbled, swiping a hand across his forehead. "Rebecca, are you sure we're reading that thing right?"

My grip on the map tightened, and I felt the sting of defensiveness rise in my chest. "I'm following Jeremiah's notes exactly. If anyone has a better idea—"

"Maybe if you'd let someone else take a look," he snapped back, his patience fraying at the edges.

Dr. Bellamy, usually lost in thought or jotting down notes in her leather-bound journal, paused and peered over her glasses at us. "Children, please. This bickering is counterproductive."

I could feel my face flush with frustration. Isaac had always been the adventurer, the one who knew how to navigate the stars and read the land. And here I was, trying to lead when it wasn't my nature.

Isaac took a step closer. "We're wasting daylight because of your stubbornness. You think you're always right because this is your family's crazy quest."

The words stung like thorns, each one a prick to my already wavering confidence. I fought to keep my voice steady. "This isn't about me being right; it's about finding the Amulet and breaking the curse."

"Enough," Dr. Bellamy cut in sharply before Isaac could retort. "We are all tired and on edge. Let's remember Penelope's words about empathy—about understanding each other's burdens."

She stepped between us, her gaze softening as she looked from me to Isaac. "Rebecca carries a heavy weight—the hopes of her ancestors and the fear of failing them. And Isaac," she turned slightly to include him in her compassionate stare, "you're worried for her safety as well as your own desire for adventure."

Isaac's shoulders slumped slightly under Dr. Bellamy's gentle reprimand.

"We can't lose sight of why we're here," she continued, reaching out to fold the map in my hands gently. "Let us not be enemies when our true adversary is still out there, seeking to claim what we must protect."

Her words hung in the air like mist—ethereal and cleansing—washing away some of the tension that had built between us.

I met Isaac's gaze; his blue eyes held an apology that didn't need words.

"Let's take a break," I proposed, my voice carrying the weight of not just our physical exertions, but the emotional toll of our journey as well.

Dr. Bellamy nodded in approval as we found a small clearing and settled down on the ground, our backs against cool tree trunks.

"We'll figure this out," I murmured more to myself than to them.

"We will," Isaac agreed after a moment, his earlier fire quenched by Dr. Bellamy's timely wisdom.

The silence that followed wasn't awkward but rather filled with reflection as we each considered our roles in this shared journey—a journey that had started with an old diary and an even older family legend but had become so much more for each of us.

We rested there until our breathing slowed and our spirits lifted enough to consider moving forward once again—united by our mission and by the understanding that empathy would be our guiding light through darker times.

I wiped the sweat from my brow, the dense foliage of the jungle making the air thick with humidity. Isaac pushed aside a large leaf, revealing a clearing that took our breath away. Before us lay a vast expanse of water, so clear and still it mirrored the sky above, a perfect circle nestled among the trees.

Dr. Bellamy stepped forward, her eyes wide behind her glasses. "This...this is the Mirror Pool," she whispered, awe lacing her voice. "Legend says it reflects not just your face but your soul's truest desires."

Isaac chuckled, breaking the reverent silence. "What does my soul desire? Probably a cheeseburger after all this trekking."

Despite his jest, I saw him peer into the water, his expression softening as he gazed at his reflection.

I approached the pool's edge, kneeling to let my fingers graze the surface. Ripples cascaded outward, distorting our reflections before settling back into a perfect stillness. It was as if time stood still around this natural marvel.

"Imagine," Dr. Bellamy said, "the countless travelers who must have stopped here over the centuries, searching for answers or simply marveling at its beauty."

I could almost hear Penelope's voice in my head, gentle and firm. "Remember," she had said to us before we left her quaint town, "the journey will show you wonders if you're open to seeing them. Let them remind you why you're here."

We stood there in silence, each lost in thought, until Isaac finally spoke up. "You know," he began, his voice softer than I'd heard it before, "I didn't expect to find anything like this out here. It's easy to get caught up in maps and puzzles and forget we're walking through a world full of miracles."

Dr. Bellamy nodded in agreement. "It's moments like these that history books can't capture." She turned to me with a gentle smile. "What does your reflection tell you?"

I looked into the water again, seeing my own eyes staring back at me with a newfound clarity. I thought of Eleanor and Jeremiah's stories that had fueled my dreams as a child and now propelled me on this quest as a young woman.

"It tells me that we're on the right path," I said.

Our collective moment by the Mirror Pool reignited something within us—a shared sense of wonder that had been dulled by fatigue and constant vigilance on our journey. The amulet's lore had become real in that moment of reflection; it wasn't just about breaking curses or finding artifacts—it was about discovery and connection.

As we left the pool behind us and continued through the jungle with renewed purpose, I could feel our resolve solidifying with each step we took together. Penelope's words echoed not just in my mind but in my heart—this journey was more than our own; it was a tapestry of lives woven together by fate and choice alike.

We moved forward as one, united by awe and wonder at what lay ahead.

We trudged through the underbrush, our breaths mingling with the mist that clung to the early morning air. Penelope's lore, a blend of whispered tales and heartfelt advice, guided us to a moss-covered archway half-concealed by wild ivy. I reached out, fingers tracing the ancient stone that beckoned us closer, feeling a connection as if the archway itself was an old friend whispering secrets.

"This has to be it," I said, my voice steady despite the thunderous beat of my heart. Isaac nodded, his eyes reflecting the same mix of determination and awe that I felt.

Dr. Bellamy removed her glasses, wiping them on her shirt before replacing them on her nose. "Indeed," she murmured, studying the archway with an academic's scrutiny. "Penelope's description was spot on."

The hidden entrance was just as she described – a silent guardian of history, standing watch over secrets untold. The chill of anticipation crept up my spine as we crossed the threshold.

Inside, we were met with a labyrinth of shadow and stone. Our footsteps echoed in the hollowness of the corridor as we ventured deeper into the heart of mystery.

"Stay alert," Isaac breathed in a hushed tone, his breath short. "Challenges often have more to them than meets the eye."

The first trial came in the form of an ancient inscription etched into a wall, lines weaving together like threads in a tapestry. Dr. Bellamy's expertise shone as she deciphered the cryptic text.

"It speaks of honesty," she explained. "A reminder that truth is often hidden beneath layers of deceit."

I thought about my family back home, how I had slipped away without a word. Was it deceit? Or was it self-preservation? The line between the two blurred in my mind.

Next came a chamber where shadows danced across walls inscribed with riddles that teased our intellects. Isaac proved his worth here, his adventurous spirit untangling the wordplay with surprising ease.

"I've always liked puzzles," he admitted with a grin that reached his eyes for the first time since we'd started this journey.

We progressed through challenges that tested our trust—a precarious bridge over an abyss that required us to depend on each other's judgment; an optical illusion that could only be solved by viewing it from each other's perspectives; and finally, an ethical dilemma posed by lifelike statues poised in silent judgment around a golden chalice.

"The test is clear," Dr. Bellamy said after reading an inscription at the base of one statue. "Take from another only what you would freely give away."

Isaac reached for the chalice but paused, hand hovering above it. His eyes met mine, questions and understanding passing silently between us.

I nodded once and Isaac withdrew his hand without touching the artifact. We walked away from temptation, leaving it untouched and proving ourselves worthy in whatever unseen eyes watched us.

Finally, we entered a domed chamber, illuminated by the flickering light of flaming torches, which exposed a central dais. Resting upon it was a piece of the Austral Amulet, radiating an energy that throbbed in sync with my innermost self.

"It's beautiful," I breathed out, captivated by its ethereal glow.

Dr. Bellamy approached cautiously, gloves now protecting her hands as she examined it from all angles without touching it directly.

"More than beautiful," she corrected. "It's powerful. Can you feel it?"

I did feel it—a call that was almost audible, beckoning me forward.

Isaac watched with cautious apprehension, but made no move to stop me as I approached the altar, my hand outstretched toward the coveted Amulet piece. Despite the tremble in my fingers, it wasn't fear that coursed through me, but a sense of anticipation and purpose. This was the culmination of our quest, the very essence of what we had been seeking—what I had been seeking since the moment I first laid eyes on Eleanor's diary.

As my skin made contact with the cool metal of the Amulet piece, a surge of warmth flooded through me—like sunlight breaking through clouds after a stormy day.

"We've done it," I said, voice thick with emotion as I lifted my gaze to meet those of my companions. "We've found it."

Dr. Bellamy gave a grave nod as Isaac patted my back, his touch conveying both fellowship and solace.

Isaac, bent forward and looking spent, took a moment of solitude.

"The third piece," Dr. Bellamy whispered as she finally allowed herself to touch it—a historian making contact with history itself.

Each piece we'd collected so far had been unique—a testament to their individual histories and powers—but this one felt different; more ancient somehow and undeniably significant.

We took a moment there in that sacred space—three souls bound by fate and determination—to appreciate what we had achieved together before gathering ourselves for what lay ahead.

"We should move on," Isaac suggested after some time had passed in reflective silence. "Before someone else finds us here."

He was right; lingering wasn't an option—not when every second could bring Anton or others like him closer to our trail.

With careful hands, Dr. Bellamy wrapped the Amulet piece in cloth before placing it securely in her bag alongside its counterparts. The weight of our discovery—and all it represented—settled between us like a new member of our unlikely family.

We exited the chamber as silently as we had entered, leaving no trace behind except for footprints soon to be swept away by time or chance visitors following their own stories yet untold.

Chapter 11

Departing from the room containing the third fragment of the Austral Amulet, a wave of victory washed over me. Isaac and Dr. Bellamy flanked me, their expressions carved with a mix of weariness and thrill. Our journey had been a series of enigmas and trials, leading up to now, and as my fingers grazed the icy surface of the metal in the room, it was as if I were making contact with the annals of time.

Isaac exhaled deeply, his gaze dropping to the floor, and I observed a faint quiver in his hands. It struck me as peculiar; he had always appeared as a steadfast boulder throughout our chaotic quest.

"Guys," Isaac's voice cracked as he broke the silence. "There's something I need to tell you."

Dr. Bellamy and I exchanged glances before turning our full attention to him.

"Since childhood, I've experienced these... moments," he began, his eyes evading ours. "My father disappeared when I was just a boy. It devastated me. Occasionally, I'm seized by this sudden dread, as if I'm suffocating and everything is converging on me." "Up until this point, I managed, only occasionally short of breath, but now my pulse quickens and a touch of terror is creeping through me. Perhaps it's because of the memory that resurfaced earlier, the one where my dad falls—a nightmare that's haunted me repeatedly."

The admission hung heavy in the stale air of the cavern. It was as if Isaac had laid bare a part of his soul none had seen.

I recalled the distance that had grown between us, years when our childhood adventures became just memories. I'd never understood why until now.

"You're talking about panic attacks?" Dr. Bellamy asked, her tone warm with concern.

Isaac nodded, his blue eyes meeting mine for the first time since his confession. "Yeah," he whispered.

"Why didn't you tell me?" My voice was barely above a whisper.

"I was scared," he admitted. "Scared you'd see me differently... less than... that you wouldn't want to be around someone broken."

"Isaac," I said, stepping closer to him, "you're not broken. And you're one of the bravest people I know."

He chuckled without humor, running a hand through his sandy blond hair.

"I don't feel brave," he confessed. "Most days it's a battle just to keep it together."

I saw Dr. Bellamy move closer as well, her presence comforting.

"Isaac," she said, "acknowledging your fear takes more courage than most people muster in their lifetimes."

Her words seemed to ease some of the tension from his shoulders.

"Look at what you've done on this journey," I continued, gesturing around us at the cavern walls that held history and secrets. "You've faced down everything that's been thrown at us."

"Yeah," he breathed out a laugh that held more truth this time. "Guess I have."

Dr. Bellamy smiled behind her glasses, pride evident in her gaze.

"And you've been doing it while battling these panic attacks? That's remarkable," she said with sincerity.

It struck me then how much we all hid beneath our surfaces; our fears and insecurities locked away like the pieces of the amulet we were collecting.

Isaac's vulnerability bridged a gap between us that had been widening since Eleanor's passing—since we embarked on this journey not just to find an artifact but to discover parts of ourselves along the way.

"You've come so far," Dr. Bellamy continued, placing a supportive hand on Isaac's shoulder. "We both admire your strength and resilience."

"And we're here for you," I added. "No matter what happens."

Isaac met my gaze again and this time held it; something unspoken passed between us—a new understanding forged from shared hardships and newfound trust.

"I can't promise I won't have another attack," Isaac said after a moment, his voice stronger now. "But knowing you guys have my back... it means everything."

As Dr. Bellamy nodded her approval, there was a profound sense of determination settle within me, strengthening my resolve even further.

"We're in this together," I stated with conviction.

The weight of his secret seemed to lift from him slightly as he stood taller beside us—less like someone carrying the world alone and more like part of a united front ready to face whatever lay ahead.

We lingered in that moment of solidarity before gathering ourselves for what came next—three pieces found but more still hidden away waiting for us to bring them into the light.

Throughout this quest, every shard we uncovered drew us nearer to not only shattering an age-old hex but also to a deeper comprehension of one another—and our own identities—more profound than ever previously experienced.

We climbed out from under the earth's surface back into daylight with our spirits bolstered by newfound truths: that courage could be found in admitting fear; strength could be drawn from vulnerability; and bonds could be forged stronger than any metal by simply standing together in honesty and trust.

Anton Kozlov stood at the edge of a windswept cliff, his silhouette stark against the dying light of day. The wind tugged at his coat with icy fingers, but he barely noticed, his dark eyes fixed on the horizon. His jaw clenched in a manner that suggested a tempest brewing within, mirroring the gathering storm clouds above.

He had been so close, mere hours behind them at every turn. His informants scattered across the region had fed him snippets—sightings of an old van, hushed conversations about a trio asking questions that were too pointed to be casual. Yet, with each lead pursued, he found himself grasping at shadows.

A phone call had just ended; another dead end. The informant's voice still echoed in his ear, tinged with the uncertainty that fueled Anton's frustration. He crushed the phone in his hand until the screen splintered, its electronic lifeblood seeping between his fingers.

"They're toying with me," he muttered under his breath. He didn't truly believe they were intentionally evading him—they lacked his cunning for such games—but the result was the same. It gnawed at him.

He turned away from the abyss, his coat whipping around him like a dark flag. "We change tactics," he spoke to the man who stood a respectful distance behind him, waiting in silence. Anton's voice held a new edge of determination. "They can't hide forever."

The man nodded once, understanding that failure was not an option.

The sun had long set when we pulled over for a rest. Dr. Bellamy insisted we stop; my eyes had started to betray me, struggling to stay open as we navigated unfamiliar roads. I didn't argue—there was something about nightfall that made our journey feel more precarious, like each shadow could conceal danger.

As Dr. Bellamy and I discussed our next move on the side of the road, using hushed tones as if afraid to disturb the peace of night, Isaac wandered off into the darkness for some air. He needed these moments alone sometimes; I understood that well enough.

It wasn't long before we heard a rustle from the underbrush—a subtle sound that might've been dismissed as an animal if we hadn't all been strung tight as bowstrings. We froze, each of us exchanging glances that conveyed a singular thought: we weren't alone.

"Stay here," Isaac whispered and moved toward the sound with a stealth I hadn't known he possessed.

My heart thundered in my chest, its rapid beats threatening to betray our presence. Desperately, I clutched at the pendant Eleanor had bestowed upon me, its familiar weight serving as an anchor amidst the chaos, grounding me in the moment.

Shortly thereafter, Isaac came back, his eyes wide and vigilant. "We have to leave—immediately," he urged in a hushed voice.

Dr. Bellamy didn't hesitate; her trust in Isaac was absolute. We swiftly gathered our gear and rejoined the road, the travel guides (who had been awaiting us) piloting the old van, its tires churning over the gravel.

We drove in silence until Isaac's breathing grew erratic—a rhythm I recognized all too well.

"Isaac?" My voice broke through the quiet like shattered glass.

"I'm okay," he managed between breaths that were too shallow and too quick.

Dr. Bellamy reached over from the backseat and placed her hand on his shoulder—a gesture meant to ground him as much as my pendant grounded me.

"Concentrate on your breaths," she instructed with authority. "You're not alone."

Isaac clutched the dashboard more firmly, as though it was the sole anchor preventing him from being swept away by his terror of succumbing to panic.

The confrontation with whatever—or whoever—had lurked in those shadows had brought his fear to life like kindling to flame. But even as he fought his internal battle, I saw something remarkable: he pushed through it because we had come to depend on him.

The adrenaline eventually waned enough for us to consider our circumstances more fully. We'd escaped immediate danger but now faced a truth we couldn't ignore: Anton Kozlov wasn't merely shadowing us anymore; he was hunting us with relentless intent.

"We have to assume they'll keep coming," Dr. Bellamy remarked, her voice low and tinged with urgency, once we had found refuge in another makeshift hideout—a dilapidated motel at the edge of civilization, its very existence shrouded in mystery.

"We've been careful," I countered, though doubt crept into my voice uninvited.

"Not careful enough," Isaac added after regaining some semblance of calm post-panic attack. "They found us tonight."

I pondered this new reality where every stranger could be an agent of Kozlov's, every turn could lead into a trap... It was like living inside one of Eleanor's stories—except this time there was no promise of safety within the final pages.

We agreed then, our voices low and determined against the backdrop of an ominous night: caution would be our constant companion from here on out; trust would be given sparingly if at all; and every step forward would be taken with eyes wide open for fear of what lurked just out of sight.

We settled into our respective corners of our temporary haven—not quite comfortable enough to sleep deeply but too exhausted not to try—and let silence fall over us like a shroud. But even in sleep's embrace, my dreams twisted with unease—the kind that comes when you know you're being pursued, and your journey has become more than just finding pieces of an ancient amulet; it's become about surviving long enough to put them together.

Chapter 12

The aged vehicle's motor droned a dull serenade while we nestled under the faint illumination of the instrument panel. Beyond the windows, the night was a dark canvas punctuated by sporadic twinkles of stars. Isaac occupied the co-driver's seat, his gaze shifting to the rearview mirror more frequently than the path forward. Dr. Bellamy's spectacles caught the minimal light as she scrutinized our wrinkled chart, her digit navigating potential paths akin to a conductor leading a silent symphony.

"We can't keep driving in circles," I murmured, my voice barely rising above the thrum of the engine. "Anton and his cronies are probably tracking us by now."

Isaac nodded, his jaw set. "We need a decoy, something to throw them off our scent."

Dr. Bellamy removed her glasses, polishing them on her sleeve before replacing them on her nose. "If we're dealing with someone as cunning as Anton Kozlov, it won't be easy. He's likely anticipating our every move."

I clutched the pendant hanging around my neck, Eleanor's face flashing in my mind. Her stories had always been filled with clever escapes and ruses. Now it was our turn to create one.

"We could split up," I suggested tentatively, unsure of how they'd take it. "It might confuse them long enough for us to gain some ground."

Isaac tapped rhythmically on the dashboard, mulling over the idea. "Dividing our forces might be effective. We just have to approach it intelligently."

Dr. Bellamy leaned forward, her eyes sharp with intellect. "We have an advantage—they don't know we're onto them yet. Let's use that."

A plan began to form, and with it, a sense of control seeped back into me.

"We have three pieces of the Amulet already," I said, my confidence growing with each word. "Let's make them think we're going after the forth one straight away."

Isaac caught on quickly. "But instead, we'll circle back and cover our tracks."

Dr. Bellamy unfolded another section of the map and pointed to a dense forest area that could easily conceal our movements.

"The forest will give us cover," she said decisively.

We spent the next hour devising our strategy—setting up false trails and utilizing every trick in the book to mislead Anton and his team.

I could feel the tension mounting as we put our plan into action; a cat-and-mouse game where the stakes were life-changing artifacts and perhaps even life itself.

The first rays of dawn were painting gold streaks across the horizon when we enacted our plan.

"Remember," Isaac said as he adjusted the rearview mirror one last time, "stick to what we agreed upon. No heroics."

Dr. Bellamy nodded firmly while I swallowed hard against the lump in my throat.

"See you all on the other side," I whispered more to myself than anyone else.

We split up at an old service station that looked like it hadn't seen business in decades—Isaac taking off on foot into a copse of trees while Dr. Bellamy and I doubled back in the van with our guide at the wheel.

Every bump in the road sent jolts through my body; every turn made my heart race faster than before.

The sensation of being hunted had become palpable, a relentless predator lurking just beyond the periphery of our awareness, its presence felt with every beat of our hearts.

We moved with caution, each step weighed down by the knowledge that danger could strike at any moment, waiting patiently for the slightest misstep to pounce upon us.

Our guide maneuvered through back roads and hidden paths known only to locals like him—his trusty van groaning under its own weight but never failing us.

"We'll drop little breadcrumbs for them," Dr. Bellamy said, her voice steady despite the situation. She pulled out old clothes from her bag and scattered them at random intervals along our path—red herrings that would hopefully buy us more time.

Every fiber of my being was stretched taut with stress but tempered by determination; this was no longer just about finding pieces of an amulet or breaking some age-old family curse.

It was about proving to myself that Eleanor had been right about me—that beneath this quiet exterior lay a heart bold enough for adventure and strong enough to face whatever came its way.

As daylight broke fully over us, turning skies from lavender blushes to azure clarity, we found ourselves deep within a thicket where no prying eyes could easily find us.

"This should be far enough for now," our guide said as he killed the engine—the silence that followed felt both oppressive and comforting.

Dr. Bellamy consulted her map again while I stepped out into the crisp morning air—a temporary respite from our relentless chase.

"We'll rest here for a few hours then keep moving," she instructed, always thinking two steps ahead.

I nodded silently before finding a spot near a tree where I could sit down and let my racing thoughts catch up with me—each beat of my heart a drumroll to action and resolve that had brought us this far.

And somewhere out there, Isaac moved like a shadow among shadows—our brave decoy in this high-stakes game we were all too invested in to lose now.

———— · ◦ ◉ ◦ · ————

The sun had shifted in the sky, casting long shadows across the rugged terrain as we set off again. Our guide, Milo, a grizzled man with an intuitive sense of direction, took the wheel of his old van, manoeuvring through the less traveled roads with a kind of casual expertise that spoke of years spent navigating these parts. Dr. Bellamy sat beside him, her gaze frequently scanning the maps spread out on her lap, while I prepared our little diversions.

We'd become adept at leaving false clues, breadcrumbs that would lead Anton and any other would-be followers astray. It was a game of wits—a trail of campsite remnants scattered miles from our true path, notes in public logs signed under aliases, and casual conversations with locals about fictional destinations.

Isaac excelled at this game too; he moved like a shadow when setting up decoys, slipping in and out of sight with a silence that belied his solid frame. He had learned the art of stealth out of necessity—his panic attacks often triggered by attention—and now it served us all.

Circling back to the origin of our ruse, a recognizable figure appeared; Isaac had finished his clandestine task, and the decoy stood finished.

I found my own role in decisiveness. Choices that once seemed mountainous now appeared before me as mere stepping stones. Each decision was a firm press into the earth beneath me—whether to trust a stranger with our true direction or to take the left fork in the road rather than the right. The weight of leadership rested easier on my shoulders with each passing day.

Dr. Bellamy's knowledge was our compass. She wove together history and lore with an academic precision that turned old tales into guides. She could read the land like one reads a book—each chapter telling her where we had to step next.

We had turned evasion into an art form; it became part of our routine as much as setting up camp or sharing stories by firelight. But even the best-laid plans have their faults.

As the day waned, we arrived at a lively market within a diminutive settlement nestled against a sharp incline.

Our pact was to replenish our stores here—swiftly and inconspicuously. Our guide halted at the market's outer edge, and we divided our efforts once more: Isaac and I to gather supplies, Dr. Bellamy to seek out regional historical texts or charts that might serve our purpose.

Isaac and I moved through the throngs with ease, filling our basket with essentials. We were almost done when I caught sight of something—or rather someone—that made my heart lurch.

At a stall selling vintage jewelry not unlike those pieces from Eleanor's stories, stood a woman who seemed familiar. Her eyes darted around as if she were searching for someone—searching for us? I nudged Isaac and nodded subtly toward her.

"Let's circle back," I whispered.

Without questioning me, he nodded, and we retreated into an alleyway that ran behind the stalls.

Dr. Bellamy wasn't so fortunate.

When we found her again, she was surrounded by a group of curious onlookers, drawn by her interest in an old map laid out before her on a vendor's cart.

"Dr. B," I called out as casually as I could manage, "we should be going."

She glanced up at me, eyes widening slightly as she took in my urgency. Quickly folding the map and handing over some coins, she excused herself from the gathering crowd.

As we made our way back to where our guide waited with running engine, I felt eyes upon us—not just one pair but many. Whispers seemed to follow us like shadows stretching out from beneath each stall and awning.

"We've been made," Isaac muttered under his breath.

I looked around at the sea of faces—a blend of curiosity and suspicion met my gaze from every angle.

Dr. Bellamy leaned in close as we walked briskly away from the market square. "That map," she breathed, "it's not just any old parchment—it's a fragment from Jeremiah's time."

My mind raced—had someone recognized it? Recognized us?

Our guide, Milo, sensed our tension as soon as we clambered into the van; he wasted no time speeding away from what had become too much attention for comfort.

"We'll need to be more careful," Dr. Bellamy said once we were safely away from prying eyes and ears. "Our pursuit is closer than we thought."

Isaac glanced back through the rear window, scanning for followers with a furrowed brow before turning to me with determination etched onto his features.

"We've been playing defense too long," he stated. "It's time we took control."

And so we drove on, hearts pounding not just from fear but also from resolve. We were more than wanderers now—we were hunters in our own right, chasing down pieces of history while eluding those who sought to chase us down in turn. The road ahead was fraught with uncertainty but brimming with promise; every obstacle an opportunity to prove ourselves anew.

The trusty old van rattled and hummed as we navigated the bends and bumps of the narrow road leading into the next town. I sat beside Dr. Bellamy, my hands clasped tightly around the strap of my bag, which housed the Amulet pieces we'd painstakingly gathered. Isaac kept a vigilant eye on our surroundings, his instincts as alert as ever.

Our guide, Milo, had been a godsend, or so we thought. His easy smile and knowledge of the backroads had given us a sense of security. That was until we caught sight of a pair of Anton's men lurking near the town's entrance. My heart plummeted when I saw Milo exchange a nod with them, his eyes avoiding ours immediately after.

Betrayal stung sharper than I imagined. We'd been careful to leave false trails, to stay off the grid, yet here we were, exposed by someone we'd trusted.

"We need to get out," Isaac whispered fiercely, reaching for the door handle.

"No sudden movements," Dr. Bellamy cautioned, her voice steady despite the danger. "We don't want to escalate this."

We played it cool, pretending not to notice the traitorous exchange as Milo pulled over at a small marketplace. The moment we stepped out of the van, he sped off with our backpacks still in the trunk.

I fought back tears of frustration. The pieces of the Amulet were safe with me, but our supplies were gone. We stood there, in the midst of the bustling market, vulnerable and stranded.

Isaac clenched his fists. "We can't stay here. Anton's men will be on us any minute."

Dr. Bellamy scanned our surroundings before locking eyes with me. "Rebecca, you've led us this far brilliantly. What do you suggest?"

I took a deep breath, trying to quiet the panic rising within me. We needed a plan—and fast.

"There has to be someone here who can help us," I said more confidently than I felt.

Just then, an older villager approached us hesitantly, his eyes kind but worried. "You... trouble?" he asked in broken English.

"Yes," Isaac responded without hesitation. "Our driver—he betrayed us."

The man frowned deeply before beckoning us to follow him through a narrow alleyway away from prying eyes.

"My name is Tomas," he said as we walked briskly. "I saw what happened with your driver."

Tomas led us to his modest home at the edge of town and ushered us inside before anyone could see where we'd gone.

"You need transport?" he asked once we were safely behind closed doors.

"We do," Dr. Bellamy replied graciously. "But we have no way to pay you right now; all our money was in those backpacks."

Tomas waved off her concern with a gentle smile that didn't quite reach his eyes—a man who'd seen too much but still chose kindness.

"I help," he said simply. "Not right what driver do."

Gratitude swelled in my chest; even after betrayal had nearly broken our spirits, hope arrived in Tomas's simple offer of help.

"Thank you," I said earnestly.

Tomas disappeared into another room and returned with keys jingling in his hand.

"A Jeep ," he explained. "Old but strong."

Isaac's eyes lit up with renewed purpose as he accepted the keys from Tomas's outstretched hand.

"We won't forget this kindness," Dr. Bellamy assured him warmly.

With that promise hanging in the air between us and Tomas nodding solemnly in understanding, we prepared to set out once more—wary but not defeated, thanks to the unexpected generosity of a stranger who'd become an ally in our quest for justice and truth.

I sank into the passenger seat of Tomas's Jeep, exhaustion seeping into my bones like a heavy fog. Isaac assumed the driver's seat, his grip on the wheel steady and resolute, a reassuring presence amidst the turmoil swirling in my mind. In the back, Dr. Bellamy settled into her seat, her eyes briefly closed as if seeking a moment of respite from the chaos that had engulfed us.

"Thank you, Tomas," I murmured as we pulled away from the villager who'd come to our aid. His nod was all the assurance we needed; we weren't alone in this, not completely.

The road stretched before us, dusty and winding through a landscape that seemed to hold its breath. We drove in silence, each lost in our own reflections of betrayal and trust. Isaac navigated the truck with an ease that belied the tension in his shoulders.

It wasn't long before a jarring sight snapped us back to reality—an old van, crumpled against the embrace of a ditch. It was Milo's van. The same van that should've been leagues away by now, carrying word of our whereabouts to Anton's men.

"Milo," Dr. Bellamy whispered from behind me.

Isaac brought the truck to a halt, and we stepped out cautiously. There he was, Milo himself, slumped against his overturned vehicle, a trickle of blood marring his brow.

Despite everything—the lies he'd fed us, the trust he'd shattered—my heart clenched at the sight of him: defeated, hurt.

We approached with wary steps, our shadows stretching long and thin across the ground.

"Milo?" Isaac called out first. "You okay?"

The man lifted his head with an effort that seemed to drain what little strength he had left. "I... they came after me," he rasped.

Dr. Bellamy crouched beside him, her historian's hands surprisingly adept at assessing his injuries. "He needs bandaging," she announced after a moment.

I knelt on Milo's other side and rifled through our supplies for a first aid kit we'd packed earlier. My hands worked on autopilot, cleaning his wounds with gentle swipes while my mind raced with questions. Why had Anton's men come after him? What did it mean for us?

As I wrapped a bandage around Milo's head—a crude but effective dressing—I caught Isaac's eye. His gaze held a storm of emotions: anger for the betrayal, concern for the injured man before us, fear for what lay ahead.

We helped Milo into Tomas's Jeep, propping him up in the back seat where Dr. Bellamy could keep an eye on him.

"We can't just leave him here," I said to Isaac as we secured our baggage once more.

"I know." Isaac sighed heavily but nodded toward the road ahead. "But we can't stay either."

We climbed back into the truck, Isaac firing up the engine while I stared out at the expanse beyond us. There was no telling how close Anton's men might be or what dangers still awaited us on this treacherous path.

But as we drove on toward our next destination, I felt something shift within me—a resolve hardening like steel beneath my skin. We were on this journey for more than ourselves now; it was about history and curses and secrets buried deep within the earth.

It was about finding who we were meant to be. And no amount of pursuit or peril would deter us from that path.

Chapter 13

I gripped the wheel tighter, knuckles white, as the old Jeep rumbled down the road. The horizon stretched endlessly ahead, a tapestry of muted greens and browns blurring past. Tomas's generosity had saved us, but safety was a fickle friend. We were bound for the next piece of the Amulet, a town cloaked in secrecy and history. A perfect place for Anton Kozlov's agents to blend in and lay their traps.

Milo slumped in the back seat beside Dr. Bellamy, his forehead bandaged. I could feel Rebecca's gaze from the front seat, her eyes fixed on the rearview mirror, scanning for any sign of pursuit. Dr. Bellamy shuffled through her notes, lips moving silently as she pieced together our next steps.

"Keep an eye out," Rebecca whispered, her voice barely carrying over the hum of the engine. "This feels too easy."

Dr. Bellamy nodded in agreement. "Anton's men are cunning. They'll have anticipated our route."

The air grew thick with tension as we approached the town. Narrow streets wound like serpents between ancient stone buildings that had stood witness to centuries of secrets. It was an ideal hunting ground for those skilled in stealth and deceit.

We parked on a deserted side street, shrouded by overhanging balconies and creeping vines—a place to regroup and plan our entry into the heart of this maze.

"Isaac," Rebecca called, reaching for my hand as we exited the truck. Her touch was grounding amidst my churning thoughts.

We slinked through alleys, each shadow a potential threat, every rustle a potential alarm. Milo kept his head down, muttering apologies under his breath for his betrayal.

As we rounded a corner, we froze at the sound of raised voices—a sharp contrast to the usual hushed whispers of these backstreets. A group of men surrounded a stall where an elderly vendor cowered behind his display of colorful textiles.

"Tell us where they went!" one of the men barked, his accent foreign but his intent universally understood.

The vendor shook his head vigorously, pleading ignorance with desperate eyes.

I exchanged glances with Rebecca and Dr. Bellamy; there was no doubt—these were Anton's men.

"We should help him," Rebecca murmured, her empathetic nature battling with the need for self-preservation.

"We can't risk it," I replied. "If they see us—"

Dr. Bellamy placed a restraining hand on Rebecca's shoulder. "We'll do more good by staying free and finding that Amulet piece."

We retreated as silently as we'd come, hearts pounding with adrenaline and guilt at leaving the vendor to his fate.

Our path took us deeper into the town's heart until we arrived at an ancient library that held clues to our next destination—a whisper in Jeremiah's journal that hinted at a hidden archive within these walls.

We split up inside, scouring through dusty tomes and faded maps under the watchful eyes of stone gargoyles that lined the high shelves.

Minutes felt like hours as we searched in silence until Rebecca gasped from a distant aisle.

"I found it!" she exclaimed before quickly muffling her voice with her hand. "Jeremiah mentions a secret chamber beneath—"

Her words were cut short by a crash near the entrance—a bookshelf toppled over with a thunderous echo throughout the cavernous space.

Milo and I rushed towards the sound while Dr. Bellamy stayed close to Rebecca. As we rounded another stack of shelves, two men dusted themselves off amidst scattered literature—the same brutes from before.

Their eyes locked onto mine—cold, calculating—and I knew our presence was no longer secret.

"Split up!" I yelled as I turned on my heel and dashed back towards Rebecca and Dr. Bellamy.

The chase was on; footsteps pounded behind me like relentless drums of doom—closer now than ever before.

A maze of bookshelves became our temporary refuge as we wove between them like frantic mice evading predatory cats.

Every glance over my shoulder revealed glimpses of our pursuers—their determination mirroring Anton's ruthlessness and leaving no doubt they'd stop at nothing to catch us.

In an alcove veiled by shadows, we huddled together—breathless—our escape routes dwindling as their search closed in around us.

"They're like wolves," Milo whispered hoarsely.

"We need a distraction," Dr. Bellamy said, her eyes scanning for anything useful among our hiding spot's forgotten relics.

Rebecca nodded towards a stack of heavy books perched precariously above us—an unsteady column waiting for just a nudge to unleash chaos upon those who sought to trap us below.

With practiced stealth borne from countless hide-and-seek games played in Eleanor's attic, Rebecca reached out and gave it that nudge—a cascade of ancient texts tumbling down upon our adversaries with enough noise to cover our escape through an unnoticed rear exit.

Once outside again under open skies now painted with hues of dusk, we took precious moments to regain our composure amidst cobblestone streets now emptied by evening's approach—an eerie silence settling where market cries once rang out just hours before—a silence only broken by distant shouts from within walls that had served as both sanctuary and prison moments ago.

This narrow escape only tightened the knot in my stomach—a reminder that danger lurked behind every friendly facade within this town—a realization that innocence bore no shield against Anton Kozlov's relentless pursuit—a pursuit that left me wondering just how many more close calls lay ahead before our quest reached its end or ours did first.

We had to make it back to Tomas's old Jeep, our newfound sanctuary in the chaos. The rugged tires and faded green paint had never been a more welcome sight.

"Come on!" Isaac urged; his voice laced with urgency. We threw open the doors, not even pausing to catch our breaths before Isaac fired up the engine. Gravel spat out from under the tires as we sped away from the betrayal that still hung heavy in the air.

The next town approached quickly, a hodgepodge of old buildings and narrow streets that promised anonymity — at least for a moment. We needed to regroup, reassess our options.

Milo's head hung low in the rear-view mirror. The silence between us was a thick fog of tension and unspoken questions. We parked in a secluded alleyway behind an old grocery store, the Jeep hidden from casual onlookers.

"I'm sorry," Milo finally broke the silence, his voice barely above a whisper. "I never... I didn't think they'd..."

"It's done," Dr. Bellamy cut him off with a stern look but softened her tone as she continued. "What matters now is what we do next."

Milo nodded solemnly and leaned forward, earnestness etched across his face. "There's an old smuggler's route," he began, hesitant at first but growing more confident as he spoke. "It runs through the mountains — not many know about it anymore. It could get you close to where you need to go without drawing attention."

Isaac and I exchanged a glance. Could we trust Milo again after his betrayal? Yet there was something in his eyes now — a genuine desire to make amends.

"Tell us everything," I demanded, pulling out Jeremiah's journal from my bag.

Milo outlined the route on one of Dr. Bellamy's maps, his finger tracing over ridges and valleys with surprising detail. "There are caves you can use for shelter," he explained, "and water sources marked by stacked stones left by those who used the path before."

Dr. Bellamy jotted down notes, her brows furrowed in concentration as she cross-referenced Milo's information with her own knowledge of local geography.

Isaac looked at me with renewed hope in his eyes. "We could be back on track sooner than we thought."

I nodded in silent agreement, a surge of determination coursing through my veins. With each fragment of the Austral Amulet we had uncovered, I had felt a deeper connection to the legacy of my great-great-grandfather—a bond that only strengthened my resolve to see this quest through to its end.

With Milo's guidance etched into our plans, we set our sights on finding the fourth piece of the amulet. It was out there, somewhere among forgotten history and hidden landscapes — and it was calling us forward.

The engine of Tomas's old Jeep grumbled like an ancient beast awakened from slumber as we ventured down the old smugglers' run. Milo had suggested this route, a labyrinth of forgotten paths carved through the mountains, promising it would throw Anton and his cronies off our scent. I clutched the leather-bound journal to my chest, a tangible piece of my great-great-grandfather's legacy, as Isaac navigated the rugged terrain with an expert hand.

Dr. Bellamy sat in the back seat, her eyes scanning the horizon with an intensity that matched the furrows of concentration etched on her forehead. "Keep your eyes peeled," she reminded us. "Old routes like this are riddled with hidden dangers."

Milo, still nursing the guilt of his betrayal, leaned forward from the backseat. "This run hasn't been used for years. The risk of being followed is slim."

Milo's advice sparked a pang of gratitude within me, yet it also served as a reminder to remain cautious. Trust, I realized, was a currency that needed to be painstakingly earned back in its entirety.

The higher we climbed, the thinner the air tasted—crisp and cold, as if we were inhaling shards of glass. I rifled through Jeremiah's journal, fingers tracing the aged pages until I found the section detailing this stretch of our journey. "Listen to this," I said, clearing my throat before reading aloud.

"'As I journeyed through the serpent's spine, where rock meets sky and eagles dare to fly, I found solace in knowing that each treacherous turn brought me closer to my destiny.'"

Isaac glanced at me with a wry smile. "Jeremiah had a way with words."

Dr. Bellamy nodded in agreement. "He was more poet than cartographer at times."

We shared a collective laugh—a fleeting moment of levity that cut through the tension like a knife through butter.

As we drew nearer to our destination, Dr. Bellamy unfurled an old map from within the journal's pages—a web of lines and cryptic symbols that held the promise of our next clue. We huddled around it as Isaac kept one eye on the road and one on the parchment.

"This mark here," Dr. Bellamy pointed with a slender finger, "it looks like an ancient symbol for water. There must be a hidden spring or waterfall near our destination."

I leaned closer, studying the symbol that seemed to dance before my eyes. It was as if Jeremiah himself was guiding us from beyond the grave.

The day waned into evening, shadows growing long and deep like ink spilled across the landscape. We knew Anton would be relentless in his pursuit; his greed for the amulet was insatiable—a beast that could never be sated.

Milo broke the silence that had settled over us like dust on an abandoned trail. "We're close now," he murmured, voice barely above a whisper.

Anticipation crackled in the air, electric and palpable. My heart hammered against my ribcage with such force I feared it might break free from its confines.

Then it happened—just as dusk painted the sky in hues of orange and purple—a blockade appeared ahead: two black SUVs parked across our path with men spilling out like dark water flooding from an overturned cup.

"Get down!" Isaac barked, throwing an arm across my chest as he slammed on the brakes.

Dr. Bellamy lowered her head beneath the window's edge as Milo muttered in his mother tongue—a sequence of words foreign to my ears yet resonating profoundly within me.

With no time to lose and adrenaline coursing through my veins like wildfire, I blurted out, "The ravine! To your right!"

Isaac didn't hesitate; he swerved hard right and took us careening down a narrow path hidden by overgrown brush—so narrow that branches clawed at our windows like desperate fingers trying to hold us back.

The men behind us shouted commands lost to wind and engine roar as we bounced along this secret vein in the earth's flesh—their voices growing fainter until they were nothing more than ghosts of threats left behind.

Dr. Bellamy let out a breath she'd been holding—a soft whistle between teeth—and peeked over her shoulder to assess our escape. "That was too close for comfort."

I couldn't help but agree silently while watching Isaac navigate each treacherous twist and turn with unwavering focus.

Milo leaned forward again, patting Isaac's shoulder with newfound respect. "Good work."

As night fell around us like a curtain drawn after a performance's end, we found ourselves alone once more on this forsaken path—our enemies deterred for now but never far from thought or heel.

We stopped for just a moment—to catch our breaths and steady our racing hearts—beneath a canopy of stars so bright they seemed unreal.

"I think we've earned ourselves a little rest," Isaac said with relief washing over his features.

I nodded in agreement before adding, "And maybe some food—I'm starving."

Dr. Bellamy chuckled softly while retrieving provisions from our packs—her laughter mingling with night sounds—a reminder that life persisted even when shadowed by pursuit and peril.

We ate in silence mostly—save for occasional affirmations of our continued journey—each lost in personal reflections of what had passed and what lay ahead.

With our bellies sated and our spirits bolstered by narrow escapes and shared determination, we settled into an uneasy sleep. While one eye remained open to the realm of dreams, the other kept vigil over the flesh-and-blood companions who lay beside me, their presence a comforting anchor amidst the uncertainty of our journey.

As slumber claimed me inch by reluctant inch—I knew despite distance put between us and those who wished us harm—we were never truly safe; Anton's presence lingered just beyond sight—his desire for what we sought unquenched by failure or falter.

But tonight—we were victors however fleeting—and I clung to that triumph like life raft adrift upon stormy seas—with hope as my compass and courage as my sail—determined more than ever to see this quest through until end's own end.

Chapter 14

Morning kissed the edges of the world with soft amber light, piercing the veil of night. We stirred from our makeshift beds, eyes heavy but spirits buoyant. Today we would climb the serpent's spine, as my great-great-grandfather had penned it. I fingered the pendant around my neck, a tangible connection to the lineage that had led me here.

Dr. Bellamy examined Jeremiah's journal intently, his enthusiasm reflecting the fiery radiance of the morning's first light. Isaac, his sandy hair tousled from sleep, plotted our course on a map spread across the hood of Tomas's classic Jeep. Milo, holding onto his regret and injuries from his betrayal, edged closer to listen in.

"As I journeyed through the serpent's spine," Dr. Bellamy read aloud, her finger tracing lines of faded ink, "where rock meets sky and eagles dare to fly, I found solace in knowing that each treacherous turn brought me closer to my destiny." Her voice echoed with a reverence that bordered on sacred.

Isaac nodded. "The serpent's spine... He must've meant these mountains." He pointed at a range that loomed in the distance like the backbone of some ancient beast.

I squinted at the terrain ahead. It seemed insurmountable, a barrier of jagged peaks against the clear blue canvas above us. Yet somewhere within that rugged maze lay our next clue, another piece of the Austral Amulet that beckoned us forward.

We packed our gear with meticulous care, ensuring nothing was left behind that might aid in our ascent. The air was crisp and thin as we started up the incline; each breath I drew was a mix of cold and determination.

Isaac led the way, his steps sure despite the uneven ground beneath us. Dr. Bellamy followed, her eyes scanning every rock and crevice as if they might reveal secrets known only to those who sought them. Milo brought up the rear, his expression somber but focused.

The climb was arduous, demanding more from us than mere physical exertion. It was a mental challenge too—a test of wills against nature's indifferent majesty. My muscles screamed in protest with each step upward, but I clung to Jeremiah's words like a lifeline.

As hours slipped away and we ascended higher, the landscape unfurled beneath us like a vast canvas, adorned with earthy hues and splashes of vibrant green. Amidst the breathtaking scenery, I couldn't shake the thought of Jeremiah embarking on this very journey, solitary with his thoughts and burdened by the weight of our family's curse resting squarely upon his shoulders.

The peak loomed overhead now, an imposing gatekeeper between us and our quarry. Isaac paused at an outcropping of stone and beckoned us over.

"Look there," he said, pointing toward a narrow ledge that wrapped around the mountain's face. "That could be where he meant by 'rock meets sky.'"

Dr. Bellamy consulted Jeremiah's journal once more before nodding in agreement. "It fits," she confirmed.

Milo squinted toward where Isaac pointed. "And eagles," he murmured almost to himself.

True enough, above us circled a pair of eagles—majestic creatures who called these heights their home. They soared effortlessly where we struggled, masters of their domain.

We followed Isaac along the ledge; every step measured to avoid loose stones or treacherous falls that would mean certain doom. The ledge narrowed further until we could barely walk single file without brushing shoulders with eternity.

I felt my heart hammer against my chest—not from exertion, but from awe and fear mingling together in a heady rush. We were trespassers here in this realm of stone and sky, where human footprints were swallowed by time itself, and the weight of centuries bore down upon us like a heavy shroud.

The path twisted cruelly before us as if carved by serpents rather than wind and weathering. Yet there was beauty too in this desolation—the starkness of nature untouched by man's hand.

Then we saw it—a crevice hidden behind an overhang of rock that sheltered a spring which cascaded down into a veil of mist below us.

"This must be it," Dr. Bellamy exclaimed breathlessly as she peered into the hidden alcove where water sprang forth from stone like life itself willing itself into existence.

Isaac ventured closer to examine the area while I remained rooted to my spot on the path, overwhelmed by what lay before us.

"It looks like there could be something behind this waterfall," Isaac called back over the roar of water meeting rock far below.

Dr. Bellamy joined him at once while Milo lingered beside me—our gazes locked onto their figures silhouetted against nature's backdrop.

There was no turning back now; not when we stood so close to touching another fragment of history—another piece of my family's legacy waiting to be reclaimed from time's relentless march.

We moved forward as one unit driven by purpose forged through trials faced together on this quest—a journey that had begun with an old diary and had led us here to where eagles dared and destiny awaited with bated breath for those brave enough to reach for it.

We stood there, inches away from a breakthrough, staring at the fourth piece of the Austral Amulet, yet it might as well have been miles. Encased in a clear barrier, it shimmered mockingly at us from within its icy prison. Dr. Bellamy ran her fingers over the smooth surface, her brow furrowed in concentration.

"It's not glass," she murmured, more to herself than to us.

I exhaled a cloud of condensation onto the barrier and watched it frost over momentarily before clearing again. Isaac had already tried applying heat with a lighter we found among Milo's stash of supplies, but the flame had flickered and died against the cold that seemed to emanate from the amulet itself.

"Could be some kind of self-frosting ice," Isaac suggested, stuffing his hands into his jacket pockets to warm them. "If we chip away at it, it just appears to repair itself."

Milo leaned against the wall, rubbing his chin thoughtfully. "What about something acidic? Something that could eat through?"

Dr. Bellamy shook her head. "We risk damaging the amulet."

We stood in tense silence, the air thick with frustration that hung over us like a looming storm. I bore the weight of our journey heavily upon my shoulders—the weight of expectation, responsibility, and now, this formidable barrier that stood between us and our ultimate goal.

As we each pondered in silence, I circled the icy enclosure like a predator stalking its prey. We had overcome so much: puzzles laid out by my great-great-grandfather Jeremiah, treacherous terrain, betrayal... Yet here we were, halted by what appeared to be an insurmountable obstacle.

"Nothing in the journal about this?" Isaac asked after a while, voice edged with impatience.

I shook my head but then paused. There was something... A word that kept appearing in Jeremiah's writings—a theme throughout our journey.

"Unity," I whispered to myself before speaking up louder to catch everyone's attention. "Guys! Jeremiah wrote about unity repeatedly in his diary."

"And?" Isaac prompted.

I could feel my pulse quicken as the idea formed and solidified like ice within me. "Maybe... maybe it's not about breaking through physically."

The group turned their attention to me as I approached the barrier again. "What if... what if it's about unity? About coming together? That's been at the heart of everything so far."

Dr. Bellamy nodded slowly as understanding dawned on her face.

Isaac shrugged. "It's worth a try."

We gathered around the clear encasement and tentatively reached out our hands until each palm rested against its surface. The cold bit into my skin, but I held firm.

"Now what?" Milo asked sceptically.

"Just wait," I said.

Seconds ticked by like hours; nothing happened. Isaac shifted uncomfortably beside me.

"This is—" he started but stopped mid-sentence.

Beneath our hands, something was changing. The barrier began to fog up where our palms pressed against it as if our combined warmth—or perhaps something more—was affecting it.

A warmth not born of temperature but of connection seemed to radiate through us and into the ice or glass or whatever mystical substance held the amulet captive.

"It's melting!" Dr. Bellamy exclaimed in astonishment.

The thick layer started to thin out slowly at first but then more rapidly as if our unity was indeed its kryptonite.

"Keep pressing," I urged everyone.

Our breaths mingled in clouds above us, suspended in the crisp air as we watched in awe. What once seemed unbreakable now lay shattered at our feet, reduced to puddles by our relentless effort. Amidst the remnants of ice and snow, the only thing left untouched was the amulet piece itself, resting on a small stone pedestal that had remained hidden beneath its icy covering.

Carefully, mindful not to disturb whatever magic we had just wrought, I reached for it with trembling fingers and lifted it free from its pedestal. It was heavier than I expected—cold yet thrumming with an energy that resonated up my arm and into my chest.

"We did it," Isaac breathed out beside me.

Milo let out a whoop of joy that echoed around us before he quickly clamped his hand over his mouth remembering we weren't exactly safe out in the open with pursuers potentially nearby.

Dr. Bellamy just stared at the amulet piece in my hand with something akin to reverence in her eyes.

"We really did," she agreed.

In that moment of triumph, all thoughts of fatigue and frustration evaporated like mist under sunlight. We had faced down an impossibility and emerged victorious—not through brute force or cunning intellect but through something far simpler and infinitely more powerful: unity.

The fourth piece of the Austral Amulet was now ours to safeguard as we prepared for whatever lay ahead on this winding path destiny had set before us.

***

With the fourth piece of the amulet safely nestled in my backpack, the gravity of our quest pressed down upon me like a leaden weight. We stood atop the mountain, a conquered beast beneath our feet, but now we faced a new adversary. The wind's howl grew louder, and rain began to pierce through the thickening twilight. A shiver crawled up my spine, and I could feel the cold settling into my bones.

Isaac's eyes scanned the darkening horizon, concern etching deeper lines into his forehead with each gust of wind. Dr. Bellamy adjusted her glasses, which had begun to fog with the chilling air, and Milo rubbed his hands together for warmth, each puff of breath visible in the frigid atmosphere.

"We can't stay here," Isaac said through chattering teeth. "But this weather is turning mean fast."

Dr. Bellamy nodded. "It's risky to descend in these conditions. One wrong step could be disastrous."

The weight of the amulet pressed against my back, its presence almost palpable as if it pulsed with a heartbeat of its own. It served as a constant reminder of the arduous journey we had undertaken and the daunting challenges that awaited us on the path ahead.

Milo looked out over the ledge, his voice nearly lost in the wind. "If we wait it out here, we risk hypothermia. But going down in this—"

He didn't need to finish his sentence; we all knew the peril that awaited us on that treacherous descent.

Huddled together, we weighed our options. The rain pelted us harder now, like nature itself was urging us to make a decision.

"Remember what Penelope said about empathy," I whispered, trying to summon her warmth. "It's about putting others before ourselves."

Dr. Bellamy pulled her coat tighter around her. "If we stick together, help each other every step of the way..."

Isaac met her gaze with determination brimming in his eyes. "We'll make it down as a team or not at all."

The cold bit at us with more fervor as night clawed its way across the sky. We stood at nature's mercy—or so it seemed.

That's when Great Gran Eleanor's words floated through my mind like a leaf caught in a stream—words she whispered to me during those precious story-filled evenings that seemed a lifetime away now.

"If you find yourself where hope seems but a distant memory and you've come to your end... Surrender," she had said, her voice always gentle yet edged with an unwavering strength I'd admired. "Surrender to God because when we're at our weakest, He is strongest."

I took a deep breath, my fingers numb as I reached out for Isaac's hand on one side and Dr. Bellamy's on the other; Milo hesitantly joined in until our circle was complete.

"Great Gran Eleanor believed in prayer," I began, my voice steady despite the tremors that shook my frame. "She said there are moments when all we can do is trust in something greater than ourselves."

The wind whipped around us like a cyclone of doubt trying to break our resolve.

I closed my eyes and prayed aloud—a simple plea for guidance and protection from a girl who'd started this journey unsure of herself but was slowly finding her strength through unity and faith.

"Heavenly Father," I said as our breaths mingled together in clouds of condensation, "we're lost and afraid, but I believe You can guide us through this storm."

As the words left my lips, something within me shifted—a surrender not just of circumstance but of self.

"We ask for Your protection as we attempt to make our way down this mountain," I continued. "Please keep our footing sure and our spirits strong."

I could feel Isaac squeeze my hand—a silent affirmation—and Dr. Bellamy's grip was firm and reassuring on my other side.

Milo muttered something under his breath; perhaps he too found solace in the act despite any doubts he harbored.

We remained like that for what felt like an eternity—the mountain's roar around us and the silent strength within us growing stronger with each passing second.

When I finally opened my eyes, something remarkable had happened—the rain had lessened its assault and though darkness encroached upon us still, there was a clarity in the air that hadn't been there before.

Isaac looked around, his expression one of awe mixed with disbelief. "Did it just...?"

Dr. Bellamy removed her glasses to wipe them clean; when she put them back on, her gaze met mine with renewed vigor.

Milo released our hands but kept his eyes skyward as if searching for answers or perhaps giving thanks.

I knew then that whatever lay ahead—be it peril or providence—we weren't alone in it. Our journey down would not be easy nor without danger; however, there was hope where once there was none.

And so with hearts fortified by prayer and hands still joined in unity's bond, we took that first step into uncertainty—together.

Chapter 15

As the heavenly objects sparkled against the nocturnal void, our voyage pressed on into the depths of the ebony expanse. With each stride, the weight of recent events was inescapable. We navigated downward, step by treacherous step, our exhalations forming clouds in the biting cold. An abrupt thought yanked me back to reality. The silence was unnerving, almost serene. I braced for the sound of steps crunching on the icy terrain or the soft whispers of voices scheming our apprehension. Yet there was an absence—no trace of Anton Kozlov or his accomplices.

The absence of our pursuers sent a shiver down my spine that had nothing to do with the cold. If there was ever a time to catch us, when we were at our most vulnerable clinging to the side of a mountain, that was it. Yet, here we were at the bottom, unscathed and unnoticed—or so it seemed.

Dr. Bellamy brushed a strand of hair from her face, her expression mirroring my confusion. "Odd," she murmured, her breath forming clouds in the air.

Isaac glanced around warily. "Maybe they lost our trail," he offered, but his tone suggested he didn't believe his own words.

We moved through the darkness, guided by memory and the faint glow of Isaac's handheld light until we found Tomas's old Jeep waiting faithfully where we left it. It looked more like a sanctuary than ever before.

"Let's set up camp," I suggested. "We need to rest."

There were nods of agreement as we gathered our supplies from the Jeep. The process was mechanical; set up tents, roll out sleeping bags, and start a fire—all actions done countless times before on this journey that now felt like an endless odyssey.

As Milo tended to the fire, casting flickering shadows over his repentant features, I caught Isaac watching him with an unreadable expression. The betrayal still stung, but Isaac's inherent goodness wouldn't allow him to hold onto anger. He turned away and caught me looking.

"Big day tomorrow," he said.

I nodded, fatigue pulling heavily at my limbs as I crawled into my tent. Sleep came quickly and deeply that night; even the lurking threat of Anton Kozlov couldn't keep my heavy eyes open any longer.

Morning broke with a softness that belied the perils we'd faced. Sunlight filtered through the canvas of my tent in warm patches, and for a moment I lay still, savoring this brief respite from fear and uncertainty.

When I finally emerged, I found Isaac and Dr. Bellamy already awake, sitting by the remnants of last night's fire with steaming cups in their hands.

"Morning," I greeted them, voice rough with sleep.

"Morning," they returned in unison.

We sat together in silence for a while—each lost in thoughts about what had happened on our journey so far and what was yet to come. It was Dr. Bellamy who broke the silence first.

"We've come so far," she said, her gaze distant as she traced her finger along the rim of her cup. "It's hard to believe there's only one piece left."

"One piece," I echoed softly.

The weight of that reality settled over us like a thick blanket—only one piece remained but finding it would demand everything we had left to give both physically and emotionally.

Isaac stood abruptly, his jaw set in determination as he looked down at us. "Then let's not waste any time," he said resolutely. "We'll need all our strength for this last leg."

Dr. Bellamy nodded her agreement, her expression mirroring the determination that pulsed within me. With newfound resolve coursing through my veins, I pushed myself to my feet, buoyed by the unwavering support of my companions.

The journey had tested us in ways none of us could have anticipated—it had brought out fears we didn't know we harbored and courage we didn't realize we possessed. We had each faced personal demons along this winding path: Isaac with his secret battles against panic attacks; Dr. Bellamy stepping out from behind her books into real-world dangers; and me finding leadership within when all my life I'd felt invisible.

We packed up camp methodically—every action deliberate and infused with newfound urgency—and soon enough we were ready to depart.

As Isaac started up Tomas's old Jeep and we rumbled back onto the road less travelled by anyone sane enough to avoid it on purpose, I couldn't help but feel that same sense of unity from last night's descent still coursing through us—a bond forged by shared hardships and unspoken trust that had somehow managed to grow stronger despite everything thrown our way.

Day three of our journey to the coast broke with a splendour that almost made the preceding trials seem trivial. We had camped on a high ridge, and as dawn crept over the horizon, the sky erupted in hues of orange and pink. Below us, the sea stretched out like a vast, undulating mirror reflecting the newborn day.

Isaac stirred beside me, his breath catching as he took in the sight. "Would you look at that," he murmured, eyes wide with wonder.

Dr. Bellamy emerged from her tent, her usually stern features softened by the light show. Even Milo, who had betrayed us but since strived to make amends, allowed himself a rare smile. For a moment, our collective breaths hung suspended in the crisp morning air as we packed up the Old Jeep beneath a sky painted by God Himself.

As we drove toward the distant shoreline, spirits remained high despite the fatigue that tugged at our limbs. The sea beckoned us closer with each mile conquered, its rhythmic waves a siren call promising adventure and discovery. Amidst the weariness, there was an undeniable sense of purpose, as if our mission was not just a choice but a destiny ordained by unseen forces.

Then our world jolted to a stop—literally—as blue and red lights flashed behind us. Isaac pulled over with a heavy sigh.

"What now?" Dr. Bellamy muttered as she glanced back at the approaching officers.

I swallowed hard, fear bubbling in my stomach. We hadn't done anything wrong... had we?

Milo leaned forward from the back seat. "Stay calm," he said, though his voice betrayed his own anxiety.

The officers approached—one tall and stern-looking, the other shorter but no less severe in expression. They barked something in their language that none of us understood.

Milo responded, his words clipped and respectful. A back-and-forth ensued, with each sentence from the officers sounding more accusatory than the last.

"What's happening?" I whispered to Isaac.

He shook his head slightly, just as clueless as I was.

Milo turned to us after what seemed an eternity of discussion. "We haven't filed for journey paperwork or paid road tax," he explained with an apologetic tone. "They're demanding payment... or there will be consequences."

"But we didn't know," Dr. Bellamy protested softly.

"I know," Milo said before addressing the officers again.

Their faces remained impassive as they listened to Milo's rapid speech. The tall one crossed his arms while his partner started scribbling something onto a notepad.

Milo turned back to us once more, his face grave. "I can handle this," he said.

"How?" Isaac asked skeptically.

"I'll stay," Milo said simply. "Three days in jail for tax evasion should cover it."

I felt my heart lurch at his words—three days lost due to an oversight on our part?

"But Milo," I started to protest, "after everything..."

He raised his hand to stop me. "I owe you more than this after my betrayal." His eyes held a new kind of resolve I hadn't seen before in him. "You need to find that last piece of the Amulet."

Dr. Bellamy reached out to touch Milo's arm gently. "Are you sure?"

He nodded once, firmly.

As the officers' impatience grew evident, they gestured for Milo to exit the vehicle. With heavy hearts and a silence weighed down by the gravity of the moment, we watched as he complied, stepping out of the Old Jeep and into the custody of the authorities.

"Thank you," I whispered as they led him away—a small gesture inadequate for his sacrifice.

Isaac started up the Jeep again and we pulled away slowly, each lost in our thoughts about Milo's sudden turn from traitor to savior.

Tears stung my eyes but I blinked them back fiercely—now wasn't the time for weakness or regret; it was time for resolve and gratitude. For Milo had given us the greatest gift—time—and we couldn't waste a second of it.

Chapter 16

The sting of losing Milo lingered like the aftertaste of a bitter herb, but the warmth of the coastal town thawed the chill of our recent hardships. Isaac manoeuvred the old Jeep through the narrow streets, and I could see Dr. Bellamy's eyes scan every historic marker and quaint shopfront with a scholar's curiosity. The sea air mingled with the scents of fresh bread and roasting coffee beans, coaxing a semblance of peace from our weary spirits.

We parked near a bustling square and stumbled into a cafe that seemed to promise sanctuary. It was there we planned to pore over Jeremiah's journal once more, searching for the final clue that would lead us to the last piece of the Austral Amulet. The interior was cozy, with walls lined by bookshelves and windows that framed the picturesque harbor.

Dr. Bellamy carefully spread out the worn pages of the journal on a table tucked away in the corner, shielding them from prying eyes. Yet, despite our efforts to keep our quest discreet, I couldn't shake the nagging feeling that our journey was never truly private, that unseen forces were always watching.

As Dr. Bellamy pointed to a passage scrawled in Jeremiah's cryptic hand, Isaac leaned in close, his brow furrowed in concentration. Together, we delved into the enigmatic words, each line a puzzle piece in the larger mystery we were determined to unravel.

"Does it strike you as odd," Isaac murmured, "that these instructions seem more like riddles than directions?"

Dr. Bellamy adjusted her glasses, tracing a line of text with her finger. "Jeremiah knew this amulet had enemies. He'd only want those who truly understood his life's work to follow his path."

As we huddled together, I noticed a woman at a nearby table. Her silver hair caught the light like threads of moonbeam woven into fabric, and her piercing blue eyes seemed to observe us with more than casual interest. I nudged Isaac subtly and tilted my head in her direction.

Her gaze met mine unflinching as she approached our table with an easy grace that seemed out of place in such a simple setting. "I couldn't help but overhear," she said, her voice laced with an accent I couldn't place. "You're searching for something precious."

Isaac shifted uneasily in his seat, casting me a wary glance. Dr. Bellamy closed the journal abruptly but offered a polite smile.

"We're just discussing some local history," she replied diplomatically.

The woman—Mara—smiled knowingly and pulled up a chair without waiting for an invitation. "History is full of secrets begging to be uncovered," she said. "I find it fascinating."

Isaac leaned back, crossing his arms protectively over his chest as if shielding himself from her intense scrutiny. "And what about you?" he asked sharply. "What brings you to eavesdrop on strangers?"

Mara's eyes twinkled with an unspoken mirth that disarmed my initial suspicion. She leaned forward, elbows on the table as if about to share confidences with old friends.

"I've spent years listening to stories," she explained, "collecting them like seashells on this very shore." She paused and looked each of us in the eye before continuing. "Some stories tell us more than just history; they warn us of what lies ahead."

A shadow of doubt still danced in the back of my mind, yet the earnestness emanating from her was almost tangible. The truth in her eyes wove a compelling story, one that spoke of genuine experience and profound understanding.

Mara bore a resemblance to my great-grandmother Eleanor, blending kindness with firmness. Her gaze had caught the pendant that once belonged to Great Gran around my neck. "It belonged to my Great Gran Eleanor," I mentioned. "It's lovely," Mara replied. "I sense a deep bond between you two, and the pendant seems like a fragment of her that you keep with you." Her sincere tone made me feel a sense of trust blossoming between us.

Catching Dr. Bellamy's attention, I exchanged a subtle, affirming gesture with her – a silent agreement that there might be more to Mara's words than initially perceived.Dr. Bellamy reopened Jeremiah's journal as if reconsidering its contents in light of Mara's words. She flipped through pages until she stopped at one heavily annotated entry.

"These are more than mere warnings," Dr. Bellamy confessed with renewed focus. "Jeremiah was safeguarding knowledge."

Mara nodded slowly as if she'd known all along.

"And sometimes," she added cryptically, "to safeguard something is not only to protect it from others but also to protect others from it."

A chill ran down my spine despite the warm atmosphere of the cafe as I considered her words—a stark reminder that what we sought could be as dangerous as it was valuable.

"Would you mind taking a look?" Dr. Bellamy asked tentatively, pushing the journal toward Mara.

With delicate fingers, Mara traced the archaic symbols and foreign script that danced across the parchment before looking up with an expression that mixed concern and determination.

"The path you're treading is treacherous," Mara said. "This final piece...it's protected by more than locks or puzzles." She pointed at a phrase hidden among Jeremiah's musings—a line we had overlooked but now seemed glaringly obvious under her guidance.

"The guardianship of time," Mara translated, her voice solemn.

Dr. Bellamy exchanged a look with me—an understanding passed between us that Jeremiah had left behind more than just physical barriers; there were trials here that would test our very resolve.

Mara leaned back in her chair and fixed her clear blue gaze on me directly for the first time since joining us.

"You also carry your great-grandmother's strength," she said firmly. "It will serve you well where you're going."

Her assurance filled me with a warmth that offset the ominous undertones of her warning.

Isaac broke our silent contemplation with an exhale of resolve, standing abruptly from his chair.

"We appreciate your insight," he said to Mara sincerely despite his earlier skepticism.

Mara stood as well and offered us each a nod that held weight—a silent pact sealed without words.

"Be wary," she cautioned one last time before departing as enigmatically as she had arrived.

The three of us sat there for a moment longer in silent accord before gathering ourselves to leave—a new protagonist's warning etched into our collective memory as we faced what lay ahead in search for the final piece of the Austral Amulet.

———— • ◦ ◉ ◦ • ————

The ancient Jeep's engine rumbled with a ferocity akin to a wild animal trapped behind bars, its very core itching to launch itself down the impending slope. As the last vestiges of the town vanished from our rearview mirror, an unspoken pact seemed to envelop the interior of the vehicle, wrapping us in a thick blanket of quietude. Isaac's fingers clung to the steering wheel with a vice-like grip, his knuckles bleaching to a stark white as he navigated each hairpin twist and turn. To his right, Dr. Bellamy's forehead was furrowed with focus, her eyes darting across the well-worn pages of Jeremiah's journal, scavenging for clues or signs that might reveal what dangers or discoveries awaited us. In the rear seat, I cradled the diary, its presence a tangible echo of our mission, providing a strange blend of solace and an ever-present echo of the gravity of our expedition.

The path ahead unwound like a weathered ribbon, faded and neglected by time's indifferent march. It twisted down a slope so precipitous it appeared to plunge directly into the earth's core. We commenced our downward journey, the Jeep jerking and jostling with every uneven dip and fissure that scarred the rugged terrain.

"Watch out for that—" Dr. Bellamy's cautionary shout pierced the air a split second before a boulder emerged from the shadows, a menacing obstacle in our precarious descent.

With swift precision, Isaac twisted the wheel, his reflexes honed but the merciless road offering little quarter. Tomas's Old Jeep careened from the designated trail, convulsing us violently as it collided with an unseen object nestled within the wild, towering grasses. Abruptly, we halted, our collective breaths suspended in a liminal space between relief and burgeoning dread.

We scrambled from the vehicle's confines to survey the havoc wrought upon it. The front tire had borne the full brunt of our inadvertent detour—gashed open, rendered utterly beyond the realm of repair.

"Great," Isaac muttered as he retrieved the spare tire and jack from the back. "Just what we needed."

Dr. Bellamy folded her arms, scanning our surroundings with a furrowed brow. "At least we're all unscathed."

I observed Isaac's focused demeanor as he set up the jack, methodically preparing to lift the Jeep off its wounded limb. His movements were precise and practiced, each action performed with steady hands. However, as he began to hoist the vehicle, an ominous creaking sound pierced the air, causing a momentary pause in our efforts.

The jack gave way like a brittle bone snapping under pressure. Isaac tried to leap clear but wasn't quick enough; the Jeep lurched, and I heard him cry out—a sharp sound that clawed at my chest.

"Isaac!" I rushed to his side where he lay cradling his arm close to his body.

"It's nothing," he gritted out through clenched teeth, but his face was pale, beads of sweat lining his forehead.

Dr. Bellamy kneeled beside him, her hands moving with practiced ease as she examined his arm. "It's not broken," she said after a tense moment, "but you've sprained it badly."

Isaac tried to push himself up with his good arm but winced at even that small movement.

"What now?" I asked, my voice barely above a whisper as I surveyed our isolated surroundings—nothing but untamed wilderness for miles around.

Dr. Bellamy sighed deeply before locking eyes with me. "We fix this tire ourselves and get to that boat." Her determination was clear, even if her voice wavered slightly with concern for Isaac.

Together we managed to prop up another makeshift support for the Jeep using rocks and branches we collected from around us. With Isaac directing us through gritted teeth, Dr. Bellamy and I changed the tire—a clumsy operation marked by our inexperience but driven by necessity.

Isaac was carefully resettled into the Jeep, and we resumed our journey, Dr. Bellamy at the wheel this time. We proceeded with greater caution, each jolt from the uneven terrain drawing a strained noise of discomfort from him.

As I looked out at the untamed wilds that stretched on either side of us, I realized that no matter how prepared we thought we were, there were still trials ahead that would test us in ways we couldn't predict or understand—yet together we would face them all.

• • ❋ • •

The dock stretched out like a tired limb into the churning sea, each wooden plank groaning under the weight of our weary steps. The sky held the promise of dawn, a gentle bloom of light teasing the horizon. The boat, a sturdy vessel with paint peeling from its hull like old sunburnt skin, rocked gently, waiting to carry us to our final challenge.

Isaac winced as he shifted his weight, the bandage around his arm a stark white against his tan skin. His eyes met mine, and I saw the pain etched in the lines around them. But there was something else there too—a fierce determination not to let us down.

"We've come too far to let a little pain stop us," he muttered, more to himself than anyone else.

Dr. Bellamy placed a hand on his shoulder, her gaze stern yet kind. "You've only got one good arm now, Isaac. You must be careful."

I could tell she was worried about him, about all of us. Mara's cryptic warnings about the final piece of the Amulet lingered in my mind, echoing with every creak of the boat as we boarded.

The hull swallowed Tomas's old Jeep whole, hiding it in its belly like a secret we weren't sure we wanted to keep anymore. I watched Isaac as he navigated around the tight space with one good arm, his jaw set in silent frustration. It was clear that physically, this part of our journey would demand more from him than he might be able to give.

Dr. Bellamy caught my eye and nodded towards Isaac, her expression a mix of concern and admiration. "He's stronger than he looks," she whispered.

"I know," I replied. "But it's not just about strength."

She nodded again, understanding that Jeremiah's diary had painted this last leg as not just physically demanding but mentally torturous as well.

We found our cabins—small rooms with portholes offering glimpses of an endless blue expanse—and stowed our gear. Isaac lay on his bunk, arm propped up on a pillow while Dr. Bellamy examined it once more.

"Try not to use it too much," she advised. "Rest will help."

Isaac grimaced but nodded. We were all exhausted from navigating the treacherous roads that led us here; every bump and turn had felt like a countdown to an inevitable end—either of our journey or ourselves.

As the boat's engines rumbled to life and we began to pull away from the dock, I leaned on the railing outside my cabin door. The wind carried the scent of salt and adventure, but underneath it was the faint smell of engine oil and anticipation laced with fear.

We were so close now; one day's journey would bring us face-to-face with what we'd been seeking all along—the final piece of the Amulet and whatever trials guarded it.

I glanced back at Isaac's cabin and then at Dr. Bellamy who stood beside me watching the receding shore. There was no turning back now; we were committed to seeing this through, no matter what awaited us on that remote island.

The ocean stretched before us—a vast expanse separating us from our goal—and I felt both small and mighty in its presence. The waves whispered secrets I longed to understand as they guided us towards our destiny.

As night fell and stars began their slow dance across the sky, I thought about Eleanor and Jeremiah Harley—their stories had propelled me here—and wondered if they could see us now, if they knew how much their legacy meant.

Sleep came uneasily that night; dreams filled with cryptic symbols and warnings played behind my closed eyelids like scenes from an old movie reel.

In what felt like moments later, though it was actually hours, dawn broke across the water, painting everything in hues of gold and pink—a new day heralding new challenges and opportunities.

I found Isaac on deck staring out at the horizon where sea met sky in an indistinct line.

"How's your arm?" I asked.

He didn't turn but smiled slightly—a small tug at one corner of his mouth that didn't quite reach his eyes. "It'll get me through," he said.

Dr. Bellamy joined us then, her eyes scanning Isaac's posture for signs of discomfort or distress.

"We're strong together," she said after a moment's silence that seemed filled with unspoken words.

I looked at them both—my friends who had become family on this strange and wonderful journey—and felt an overwhelming sense of gratitude mixed with trepidation for what lay ahead.

"Yes," I agreed. "Together."

And so we watched as land faded into memory behind us while ahead lay only open water and an island that held not just a piece of ancient jewelry but perhaps pieces of ourselves we hadn't yet discovered.

* * *

The ocean's rhythmic waves lapped against the side of the boat, a soothing sound that had become a familiar companion over the past day. As I leaned on the railing, gazing into the horizon, my mind circled back to Anton and his relentless pursuit. It had been days since we last caught wind of him or his men. Their absence was both a relief and a riddle, one that nagged at me with each mile we put between us and the mainland.

"Rebecca, you're doing that thing again," Isaac's voice called out, breaking through the haze of my thoughts. He was right; I had been lost in contemplation, my gaze fixed on a distant point.

"I just can't shake this feeling," I confessed, pushing a stray strand of hair behind my ear. "Anton has been on our heels since day one. Why would he stop now?"

Isaac approached, his arm still in a sling from the jack incident. "Maybe he lost our trail," he suggested with an optimism I admired but couldn't quite share.

Dr. Bellamy joined us, her keen eyes scanning the seascape ahead. "Or perhaps he's simply biding his time," she added, her tone measured as always. "Either way, we must remain vigilant."

As we neared the island, it came into view like a gem set upon the sea's vast canvas. The island was indeed remote, more so than any of us had anticipated. From what we could see, its size was modest; traversing it wouldn't take more than a few hours on foot. Dense foliage crowned most of its landmass, with rocky outcrops piercing through here and there like ancient sentinels guarding untold secrets.

The boat's engine slowed to a gentle purr as we approached the dock—a simple structure that looked as though it had seen better days but stood resolute against time and tide. There was no sign of Anton or his men lying in wait for us—a stroke of luck or a sign of something else entirely?

"Looks like we'll have this place to ourselves," Isaac mused, leaning over to get a better look at the shore.

"Seems so," I replied, though my voice lacked conviction.

We gathered our belongings and prepared to disembark. Dr. Bellamy double-checked the supplies while Isaac made sure the Old Jeep was ready for whatever terrain lay ahead. My great-grandmother's pendant hung heavily around my neck—a constant reminder of the weight of our quest.

As we drove off the boat onto the island's sole pier, a few locals emerged from their homes to observe us with cautious curiosity. Their presence was comforting in its own way—proof that life persisted even in such isolation.

The islanders were reserved but not unfriendly; their smiles were genuine if somewhat guarded. We nodded in greeting but didn't stop to engage further—not yet at least. There would be time for pleasantries after our mission was complete.

We followed a narrow path that wound its way into the heart of the island, enveloped by lush greenery that seemed untouched by time or human hands. This place held its secrets well, but we were determined to uncover them—to find that final piece of the Amulet and complete what Jeremiah had started all those years ago.

Dr. Bellamy steered the aging Jeep across the treacherous path, with Isaac referencing Jeremiah's journal to guide us through the challenging landscape. In the back seat, I remained silent, accompanied only by my own reflections and uncertainties. Our collective journey had led us through ordeals that defied our wildest expectations, and now we found ourselves teetering on the edge of its conclusion.

Would finding this last piece change everything? Would it bring peace or merely usher in new challenges? These questions swirled in my mind like leaves caught in an autumn breeze.

But there was no turning back now; we had come too far to give up when our goal was within reach. And as I looked at Isaac's determined profile and Dr. Bellamy's focused expression, I knew that no matter what lay ahead on this remote island haven, we would face it together—as a team united by purpose and friendship.

We were ready for whatever awaited us here...

Chapter 17

The first rays of dawn crept through the foliage, casting long shadows that danced over our makeshift camp. I lay still for a moment, listening to the distant calls of unknown birds, their songs unfamiliar yet oddly comforting in this remote corner of the world. The air was thick with anticipation, and my stomach churned with a cocktail of excitement and nerves. Today was the day we'd face one of our greatest challenges yet.

Isaac stirred beside me, his injured arm carefully cradled against his chest. "Morning," he grunted, wincing as he shifted to a sitting position.

Dr. Bellamy emerged from her tent, her hair tied back and her face set in a mask of determination. "Good morning," she said, her voice steady. "Today we unravel the guardianship of time."

I pulled myself up, feeling every muscle protest after days of relentless travel. We gathered around the smoldering remains of last night's fire, the diary lying open between us. The words "The guardianship of time" stared back at us, penned in Jeremiah's elegant script.

"What do you think it means?" Isaac asked, tracing the words with his good hand.

Mara's interpretation echoed in my mind—something about cycles, continuity, and protection. But it was like trying to piece together a puzzle with half the pieces missing.

"It could be literal," Dr. Bellamy mused. "A reference to a physical place where time stands still or perhaps an object that controls it."

"Or it could be metaphorical," I added, thinking aloud. "Maybe it's about a tradition or knowledge passed down through generations."

We sat in silence for a moment, each lost in thought. It was clear that understanding this clue was crucial to finding the final piece of the Amulet.

"We won't solve this sitting here," Isaac said. "Let's get moving."

We packed up camp quickly and set out just as the sun fully broke the horizon. The island's interior beckoned us with its dense greenery, and we soon found ourselves enveloped by thick vines and towering trees.

The foliage seemed to close in around us as we trekked deeper into the island's heart. Thorns snagged at our clothes; roots threatened to trip us at every step. Sweat dripped into my eyes, stinging and blurring my vision.

Dr. Bellamy led the way, her keen eyes scouting for any hint of a trail or marker that might have been left behind by Jeremiah or those before him. Isaac followed closely behind her, his one good arm swinging a machete to clear our path through the underbrush.

The island seemed to pulse with life, every whisper of the wind and rustle of foliage magnifying in my ears until it felt as though we were enveloped in a symphony of unseen guardians, their presence palpable in the very air we breathed.

"We're on the right path," Dr. Bellamy assured us as we paused for water. "The difficulty of this terrain... it feels intentional, like it's meant to deter all but the most determined."

Isaac nodded in agreement but remained silent, conserving his energy.

With each step forward, my resolve hardened. We had come too far to let anything—man or nature—stand in our way now.

As we trekked deeper into the wild underbrush, I couldn't help but feel the weight of Jeremiah's journal against my chest. It was as if the leather-bound book pulsed with the heartbeats of past adventurers. We had barely spoken since we woke, each lost in our thoughts, perhaps pondering the same thing: would today be the day we found the final piece of the Austral Amulet?

Dr. Bellamy paused briefly to verify our route against the journal's instructions, prompting me to advance a bit to maintain our momentum, with Isaac trailing just behind, Dr. Bellamy.

The clue from Jeremiah's journal echoed in my mind: "The guardianship of time lies where the sun kisses the earth, and stone lips whisper the path to dawn's origin." I stopped abruptly, causing Dr. Bellamy to bump into me.

"Are you alright?" she asked, concern creasing her brow.

I nodded, not trusting my voice just yet. My gaze was locked on a seemingly ordinary rock face bathed in the early morning sun. I approached it slowly and ran my fingers over its surface. There it was—an intricate carving of what appeared to be a sun partially hidden by vines.

"This is it," I whispered, brushing away leaves and debris to reveal more of the design.

Dr. Bellamy and Isaac joined me, their eyes widening as they saw the carving come into full view. It matched Jeremiah's sketches perfectly—down to the smallest detail.

With excitement trembling in my hands, I pressed on a portion of the carving that protruded slightly more than the rest. A grinding noise reverberated through the ground beneath us as part of the rock wall receded and revealed an opening just wide enough for a person to slip through.

We exchanged glances, a silent agreement passing between us before we entered single file into what could only be described as an ancient vestibule. Our flashlights cut through the darkness inside, illuminating walls lined with carvings that told stories older than memory itself.

The beam from Isaac's flashlight settled on something that made him inhale sharply. "Look at this," he said with an urgency that drew our attention.

We gathered around him and saw what had captured his attention—a room filled with sun dials and ancient clocks of various sizes and designs, all frozen in time.

"The guardianship of time," Dr. Bellamy breathed out in awe.

The air around us felt charged with an ancient energy as we stepped further into the room. Each clock was positioned deliberately, their hands pointing at different hours and minutes creating a tapestry of times long past.

"We need to figure out how these relate to proceeding further," I said, studying Jeremiah's journal for any hint or instruction.

Dr. Bellamy nodded in agreement. "The time these clocks are set to must be significant. Perhaps they represent specific historical events or celestial alignments."

We split up to examine each timepiece more closely when Isaac called out from across the room where he stood by a large sun dial dominating the center of the space.

"Rebecca! Dr. Bellamy! This one's different from the others," he said while pointing at markings around its base—symbols that were neither numbers nor traditional ancient markings.

As I approached Isaac, I noticed how he gingerly moved his injured arm while still managing to participate actively in our investigation. He had come so far from that stoic façade he often wore back home; this journey had chipped away at his armor revealing his true strength beneath.

"I think these symbols represent seasons... or maybe months?" Isaac suggested, squinting at the etchings.

"That makes sense," Dr. Bellamy agreed as she joined us at his side. "In ancient times, sundials were often used to track agricultural seasons which were crucial for survival."

Isaac pointed towards an opening above us where light streamed in at just the right angle to cast a shadow from the gnomon onto one of those symbols—the symbol for harvest season if our assumptions were correct.

"We need to adjust these other clocks to align with significant moments within each season," I proposed after correlating information from Jeremiah's journal with our observations.

For hours we worked together like clockwork ourselves—Isaac using his good hand to adjust smaller mechanisms while Dr. Bellamy cross-referenced historical dates with celestial events. I took charge of documenting each setting we chose, ensuring accuracy down to the minute.

Our efforts bore fruit when a clock struck an hour unheard for centuries; its bell tolled once before silence reigned again. A portion of the wall slid away silently revealing another chamber beyond it—a hidden sanctuary within these ruins dedicated to time itself.

Isaac caught my eye as we prepared to enter this newly revealed chamber; there was a glint of pride there that mirrored my own feelings toward him. We had each grown so much since leaving Wollow Creek; none more visibly than Isaac who had conquered not only physical pain but also inner turmoil on this quest for answers and redemption.

We stood together on this precipice of discovery; three souls bound by history's call and personal resolve—a testament to human curiosity and resilience—and took our first steps into unknown history's embrace.

———— · ◦ ◉ ◦ · ————

The air in the chamber hung thick with the weight of centuries, each breath a testament to the timelessness of this place. Our footsteps echoed, a trio of heartbeats against the stone floor. Isaac, his arm cradled protectively, moved with a cautious grace born from necessity, while Dr. Bellamy's eyes scanned the walls with the voracity of a scholar starved for knowledge.

And then there was me, Rebecca Harley, standing before the walls inscribed with riddles and allegories that spoke of time's passage and family lineage. The curse's focus on bloodlines wasn't just some ghost story; it was etched into the very walls that surrounded us, whispering secrets of the past and perhaps, our future.

"Time is the river in which we all swim," I read aloud from one of the inscriptions, my voice a tremor in the silence. "Its currents are our choices, its banks are our bloodline."

Isaac approached another wall, squinting at the faded letters. "Here lies the path to unity; through trials by fire, water, earth, and air. Forged in adversity, the family stands undivided."

Dr. Bellamy joined us, her finger tracing over a series of intricate symbols that seemed to dance between being mere decoration and profound insight. "These symbols," she mused thoughtfully. "They might correspond to the elements mentioned in Isaac's riddle."

We huddled closer together as if proximity could lend us each other's wisdom or courage. The Amulet pieces we'd gathered thus far lay securely tucked away in my bag—pieces of a puzzle that had started to form a picture far greater than its individual parts.

"You know," I began, breaking our contemplative silence, "each piece we've found has brought us closer not just to completing this Amulet but to each other."

Isaac gave a measured nod. "The fire of flickering torches where the third fragment rested," he spoke in a hushed tone, his eyes reflecting a far-off recollection. "In that chamber, our presence brought the sensation of heat and comfort from one another."

Dr. Bellamy's smile emerged at the recollection, yet her gaze stayed fixed on the wall ahead. "And the water," she continued, "the subterranean river we traversed with such precision... It demanded unwavering faith in our respective skills while we journeyed that route side by side."

Emotions burgeoned within me at their declarations; indeed, each challenge encountered seemed tailored to assess and hone us. The earth served as our anchor when we delved into the planet's core, extricating the initial fragment from its sepulcher amid chambers concealed by vast networks of roots.

"And air," Isaac remarked, laughter in his voice though his arm winced at the slightest motion, "required us to jump blindly on that peak, high where the eagles soar, deftly descending the mountain's face.

We laughed together then—a short burst of shared joy amidst our shared burden—and I knew without doubt that these trials had been more than mere obstacles; they were allegories for unity and understanding.

"Perhaps that's what this is all about," Dr. Bellamy suggested thoughtfully as she returned her attention to deciphering the riddles before us. "The elements are not just trials but also metaphors for what binds a family—or any group united by a common cause—through time."

"The Amulet," I said, my fingers brushing over its cloth-wrapped form in my bag, "it's not just breaking a curse; it's showing us how interconnected we all are—how each piece is necessary for the whole."

Our reflections were interrupted by a click from one section of wall where Isaac had been pressing symbols seemingly at random. A portion of stone receded with a groan before sliding aside to reveal yet another chamber.

As we stepped through into this new space—a room where time seemed even more palpable—we were greeted by more enigmatic text wrapping around an enormous hourglass at its centre.

"This chamber... it feels alive with history," Dr. Bellamy whispered as we approached the hourglass.

Isaac glanced back at me with an encouraging nod before reaching out to touch one side of the hourglass where sand still trickled slowly from top to bottom.

"We're part of this history now," I murmured as I joined him at his side.

As each grain cascaded through the narrow passage between glass bulbs, a profound sense of inevitability washed over me. It was as if we were being inexorably drawn deeper into the intricate tapestry woven by the hands of my ancestors—a complex pattern of trials and triumphs that bound us together across time.

"The riddles here," Dr. Bellamy said as she pointed to an inscription above the hourglass that read: 'Only when time unites will bloodlines be freed.' "They're not just puzzles; they're lessons about unity across generations."

Together we worked through allegories speaking of times when families divided fell to ruin while those who stood united grew strong despite adversity.

As if in answer to our collaborative efforts, another mechanism within the chamber triggered—a soft rumble beneath our feet followed by an almost imperceptible shift in the air around us.

A new inscription revealed itself above an archway: 'To move forward through time is to understand its dance with lineage.'

We weren't just searching for physical pieces of an Amulet; we were piecing together fragments of wisdom passed down through generations—each lesson another step toward unity and understanding within our own makeshift family formed under extraordinary circumstances.

And as each riddle gave way beneath our combined intellects and intuitions, I couldn't help but feel grateful for these two people beside me—for their minds and their spirits—and for whatever twist of fate had brought us together on this journey toward something greater than ourselves.

I leaned back against the cool stone wall, feeling the weight of our journey in every bone. Isaac, with his arm cradled carefully to his chest, sat beside me. Dr. Bellamy, her eyes reflecting the dim light from our flashlights, perched on a fallen pillar, flipping through Jeremiah's journal as if it held the answers to the universe. The antechamber was a small pocket of calm in a labyrinth of trials that had tested our limits, both mentally and physically.

We were quiet for a long time, each lost in our own thoughts. The air was thick with the kind of silence that begs for introspection. I broke it first.

"We've come so far," I murmured softly, my fingers tracing the familiar contours of the silver chain around my neck—the same chain Eleanor had gifted me years ago. "From feeling invisible in a crowd to... this." With a sweeping gesture, I indicated the towering walls that whispered tales of a bygone era, each stone bearing witness to the journey we had undertaken, both outwardly and within ourselves.

Isaac nodded, shifting uncomfortably. "Each piece of the Amulet has been like a step closer to ourselves as much as it's been a step closer to breaking the curse."

Dr. Bellamy looked up from her notes. "It's remarkable, really," she said. "Each piece not only fits together like a puzzle but also seems to draw out something... essential from each of us."

The Amulet's pieces were more than just relics; they were catalysts for change. I thought about how we'd had to rely on one another's strengths to overcome each challenge—Isaac's unexpected resourcefulness, Dr. Bellamy's vast knowledge, and even my own burgeoning leadership.

"It's like they were designed to teach us something," Isaac added.

I thought about his words. Perhaps Jeremiah knew that the path to finding the Amulet would be as important as the artifact itself. Maybe he understood that unity wasn't just about putting an object back together but about bringing people together—binding them with shared purpose and understanding.

We sat in contemplative silence again until Isaac broke it with a sigh that seemed pulled from deep within him.

"I can't stop thinking about Anton," he admitted, looking at each of us with troubled eyes. "He's still out there, and he won't give up easily."

His words hung in the air like an unwelcome spectre at our campfire, reminding us that our journey wasn't just one of self-discovery but also a race against an unscrupulous adversary whose shadow loomed over us even now.

"You're right," Dr. Bellamy said gravely. "But we've outsmarted him so far, and we'll continue to do so."

I felt Isaac's fear because it mirrored my own—a fear not just for ourselves but for what Anton could do if he got his hands on the Amulet's power. The thought spurred a new determination within me.

"We'll be ready for him," I said firmly, meeting Isaac's gaze head-on. "We have something he doesn't—genuine purpose."

Isaac nodded slowly, his anxiety not quite abated but perhaps eased by solidarity.

"Yeah," he agreed. "Purpose... and each other."

<hr />

The air felt heavier as we stood before the final chamber. Dr. Bellamy held up her torch, casting light on an elaborate mechanical puzzle that sprawled across the entire back wall. Isaac leaned against the cool stone, his injured arm a constant reminder of our perilous journey. I could see the pain etched in his face, but his eyes—those were alight with determination.

The contraption before us was a labyrinth of gears and levers, a testament to ancient ingenuity and a challenge to our modern minds. It was clear that this was more than just a puzzle; it was a culmination of everything we had learned, every trial we had endured.

"This is it," I murmured, my voice barely above a whisper. "The unity we need—it's not just among us. It's... it's in everything." My hand found its way to my neck, fingers tracing the contours of the pendant Eleanor had given me years ago.

Dr. Bellamy nodded solemnly. "Unity in thought, in action, and now, in mechanism. We need to work together like never before."

Isaac pushed off from the wall and stepped forward, examining the puzzle with keen eyes. "I may have only one good arm, but I've got a working brain. Let's figure this out."

We studied the mechanism intently, noting how each gear connected to the next in an intricate dance of metal and stone. It was clear that one wrong move could reset our progress or worse, trigger a trap that would end our quest prematurely.

"Look at the symbols," Dr. Bellamy pointed out. Each gear bore an engraving—a tree, a river, a mountain—all elements of nature bound together in an ecosystem of steel.

Isaac leaned closer to a panel adorned with celestial bodies—a sun, a moon, stars arranged in patterns I recognized from Jeremiah's journal. "These must be aligned," he said confidently.

The chamber echoed with the sound of our concerted efforts as we turned dials and shifted levers. Each click and clack was met with bated breath until finally, we set the last celestial body in place.

Nothing happened.

We exchanged glances, each of us searching for missed clues or missteps. Then my eyes fell upon the pendant once more—its intricate design seemed to echo the puzzle's complexity.

"Rebecca," Dr. Bellamy urged gently, "the pendant."

With trembling hands, I unclasped the necklace and held it up to the light. The pendant gleamed as if recognizing its purpose after years of silent waiting.

A small recess in the center of the mechanism caught my eye—an empty seat amidst the network of gears where no solution seemed to fit.

"It's made for this," I said with newfound clarity.

As I inserted the pendant into the recess, it fit perfectly—as though it had been crafted by the same hands that built this ancient challenge. The gears trembled with anticipation before they began to turn slowly.

The walls of the chamber vibrated with life as if the heart of the earth itself pulsed through them. Gears interlocked with seamless precision; levers pulled themselves into new alignments; stone grinded against stone as hidden pathways within revealed themselves.

We stood in silent awe as each movement led seamlessly into the next—a harmonious chain reaction ignited by the unity embodied in a single piece of jewelry, passed down through generations as a testament to the enduring bonds that bound us together.

Isaac gripped my shoulder tightly, his breaths shallow but excited. Dr. Bellamy whispered incantations under her breath—words of encouragement or perhaps prayers from olden texts known only to her scholarly mind.

I realized then that this wasn't just about bloodlines or destiny; it was about recognizing how deeply connected we are—to our pasts, to each other, and to a world much greater than ourselves.

Sweat beaded on my forehead as I monitored every turn and twist of the mechanism, ready to intervene if necessary. But it wasn't needed; everything moved as if by magic—or rather by some divine engineering beyond our understanding but within our ability to awaken.

My heart raced; this was it—the hardest chamber indeed and yet here we were, standing together facing it head-on with courage and an unspoken trust that had been forged through fire and fear.

Isaac's gaze met mine—a silent communication that said everything: We're almost there. Don't give up now.

I nodded back at him while holding onto Dr. Bellamy's steady hand for support—the unity among us palpable and powerful enough to overcome any challenge this ancient place could conjure.

The puzzle continued its dance as if celebrating its own awakening after centuries of slumber. And there at its heart was my pendant—the key Eleanor knew I would one day need to fulfill not just my destiny but that of my entire bloodline.

We didn't dare move as we watched gears slow down their frenetic pace until they came to a deliberate stop with an echoing thud that resonated through our very bones—a final note in an orchestral masterpiece played by time itself.

In front of us stood an open passage revealed by our unity—a passage that beckoned us towards what lay beyond: The completion of our Amulet and perhaps even more than that—the completion of us all.

Chapter 18

Within the ancient structure, the culmination point of our quest, a thin beam of dwindling daylight cut through the darkness, illuminating the grand chamber unfolded before us, an immense cavity at the heart of the isle that seemed to murmur ancient secrets with every breath. We entered, our pulses racing in harmony with the resonant tapping of our steps. There it lay, cradled in a niche hewn from rock—a shimmering fragment that summoned us nearer. The concluding segment of the Austral Amulet.

Isaac's hand extended first, his recent injury lost to the rush of excitement coursing through his veins. Dr. Bellamy, ever the voice of prudence, gently laid a steadying hand upon Isaac's shoulder, her touch conveying a wordless warning. My breath caught in my throat as Isaac's fingers delicately retreated, now tenderly embracing the Amulet's gleaming piece with a reverence that bordered on the sacred. A wave of joy washed over us, so intense it was almost tangible; our eyes met in silent communion, sharing a saga of relief and victory that needed no words to be understood.

But our celebration was short-lived. The weight of responsibility settled on our shoulders like a heavy cloak. We had secured the final piece, but our task was far from complete. We needed to guard it with our lives until we could perform the ritual to break the curse—a ritual steeped in secrecy and surrounded by danger.

"We can't let our guard down," I murmured, my voice barely above a whisper. "Not until this is over."

Dr. Bellamy nodded, her eyes reflecting a wisdom that had guided us thus far. "The hardest part of our journey still lies ahead," she said solemnly.

We made our way back through the crumbling relics at a deliberate pace, stepping out into the dwindling light of day. The vibrant night-time symphony of the forest welcomed us, a vivid counterpoint to the hush we had departed from within the ancient hall.

As we navigated our way through the dense underbrush, a creeping sensation prickled at the back of my neck—a pervasive feeling that we were not alone, that unseen eyes were upon us. Judging by the furtive glances Isaac kept casting over his shoulder, his jaw set in a grim line, it was clear he shared my unease. The forest seemed to close in around us, amplifying the sense of being watched, until every rustle of leaves and every whisper of the wind felt like a harbinger of impending danger.

Dr. Bellamy remained quiet, her eyes scanning the shadows that danced between trees and vines. "Keep moving," she urged us forward with an authoritative tone that brooked no argument.

The path ahead was shrouded in darkness now, with only our flashlights piercing through like beacons guiding us home. But this island wasn't home—it was a wild place that held secrets and dangers alike.

Every snap of a twig underfoot sounded like an alarm bell in my ears. Every rustle in the foliage felt like an intruder closing in on us.

We were close to camp when Isaac halted abruptly, causing me to bump into him. "Did you hear that?" he asked, tension lacing his voice.

I strained my ears against the symphony of crickets and distant waves crashing against shorelines—nothing out of place. Yet I couldn't ignore the gnawing fear that coiled tight within my stomach.

"It's probably just an animal," Dr. Bellamy offered calmly, though she too held her flashlight like a weapon ready to be wielded.

But we all knew it wasn't animals we feared; it was Anton and his men—hunters who had proven themselves relentless and unscrupulous in their pursuit.

We huddled together for a moment longer before pressing on toward camp once more. The unease never left us; it clung to us like the humid air clinging to our skin.

When we finally arrived at camp, there was no sign of disturbance—a small mercy for which I was grateful—but I couldn't shake off the sensation that had stalked us through the jungle.

I glanced at Isaac and Dr. Bellamy as they began securing our perimeter with meticulous care—traps and alarms fashioned from whatever materials we had at hand.

We settled down around our dwindling campfire not long after, its glow warding off more than just the darkness—it kept at bay the fear that lurked just beyond its reach.

As I gazed into its embers, my thoughts wandered back to Eleanor and her stories—stories that had sparked this very journey within me. Now here I sat with her pendant around my neck and part of her legacy secured in my grasp—the Austral Amulet pieces finally reunited but still whispered promises of danger and sacrifice.

The fire crackled and popped, throwing sparks up into the night sky as if challenging stars themselves for dominance in illumination. But even as its warmth bathed us in comfort, there was no denying it: we were not alone on this island.

Our vigilance couldn't waver; even sleep seemed like an unaffordable luxury when every shadow could conceal an enemy waiting for their moment to strike.

I pulled my knees up to my chest and wrapped my arms around them tightly—as if I could shield myself from what lay ahead—and watched Isaac and Dr. Bellamy doze off in fitful starts and stops.

The night wore on while every rustle or snap of twigs sent jolts of adrenaline coursing through me—each one a false alarm but a testament to our heightened state of alertness.

Dawn would come eventually; it always did after night's reign—bringing light and clarity with it—but for now, as embers turned to ash and darkness pressed in around us like an unwelcome shroud—we were enveloped by an uneasy peace punctuated by distant howls carried on ocean breezes—a reminder that Anton's threat still loomed large over us all.

———— · ● · · ————

The first light of dawn seeped through the dense canopy of trees, casting long, spectral shadows across our makeshift camp. The chill of the morning air bit at my cheeks as I sat up, my muscles protesting the sudden movement after a night spent on the hard ground. Isaac was already awake, nursing his injured arm, and Dr. Bellamy had begun to pack up her belongings with quiet efficiency.

I glanced at Tomas's Jeep, parked a little distance away, an inert hulk in the dim light. It had been our lifeline for so long, but now it seemed almost alien—like some beast resting in the wild. The memory of last night's howls echoed in my mind, an ominous soundtrack that played on loop. They had sounded close, too close for comfort, and we had all felt it—a primal warning that sent shivers down our spines.

"Ready to go?" Dr. Bellamy asked, her voice a low whisper as if not to disturb the fragile silence of dawn.

Isaac nodded, his face drawn tight with pain and concern. I could see the shadows under his eyes; he hadn't slept well, if at all. "Let's just hope whatever made those noises last night has moved on," he murmured.

We approached Tomas's Jeep with caution that bordered on reverence. It wasn't just the howls that had put us on edge—it was the sense of vulnerability that comes with knowing you're not alone in a place where you should be.

As we neared the vehicle, it became clear that something was amiss. The underbrush around the Jeep was disturbed—leaves and twigs crushed underfoot and displaced earth that didn't match our own tread patterns from yesterday.

"Look at this," Dr. Bellamy said, kneeling to examine a set of fresh tire tracks that cut across our path. "These weren't here yesterday."

Isaac limped over to inspect them himself, wincing as he moved. "They're recent," he confirmed. "And whatever it was, it came from that direction." He pointed towards a trail that led deeper into the forest.

A knot formed in my stomach as I followed the direction of his finger. It wasn't just any direction—it was exactly where we needed to go next.

"What do you think? Hunters?" I asked, trying to keep my voice steady.

Dr. Bellamy shook her head slowly as she stood up. "I doubt it. Hunters don't come this deep into the reserve; they have no reason to."

Isaac and I exchanged glances—a silent conversation passing between us. We both knew what she meant without having to say it out loud: Anton Kozlov or his men were here, somewhere close by.

I stepped closer to the Jeep and noticed something else—a water bottle half-buried under a fern leaf not far from where we had parked. I picked it up and examined it; it wasn't one of ours.

"This isn't good," I said, holding up the bottle for them to see.

Isaac clenched his jaw tightly, his usual bravado nowhere to be seen. "They're tracking us," he said flatly.

Dr. Bellamy took a deep breath and let it out slowly before speaking again. "We need to be smart about this," she advised calmly. "We can't afford to panic or make rash decisions."

The realization crashed over me like a cold wave—the sense of being hunted was no longer a mere feeling; it was our grim reality. The tracks left behind didn't lie; someone had infiltrated our camp while we slept, their presence a chilling reminder that we were not alone. They had watched us, perhaps biding their time, waiting for the perfect moment to strike.

We stood there for a moment longer in silence before Dr. Bellamy motioned towards Tomas's Jeep once more. "Let's get moving," she said.

Isaac nodded in agreement, though his eyes kept darting back towards the trail from which we suspected our unwanted visitors had come.

As we packed our gear into Tomas's Jeep, I couldn't shake off the unease that clung to me like dew on leaves. Every snapped twig or rustle in the foliage set my heart racing; every bird call seemed like a signal alerting others to our presence.

"We can't let them catch us," Isaac said suddenly as he slammed shut the door of the Jeep after stowing away his backpack.

"No," Dr. Bellamy agreed solemnly as she climbed into her seat behind the wheel—our usual positions instinctively assumed despite everything—"we won't let them."

With one last glance over my shoulder at the quiet forest behind us—the lurking threat hidden somewhere within its depths—I climbed into Tomas's Jeep alongside Isaac and Dr. Bellamy.

As we pulled away from camp, leaving behind nothing but disturbed earth and lingering fears, I couldn't help but wonder: were we leaving danger behind or driving straight into its waiting arms?

* * *

Dr. Bellamy's hands were firm on the wheel, expertly navigating Tomas's Jeep along the rutted trail. Shafts of the early morning sun jostled for space, barely managing to slip through the lush, overhanging tapestry of leaves and vines. The silence that enveloped us was profound, almost tangible, as if our minds were adrift on separate currents of contemplation. Meanwhile, the Jeep's aged engine provided a steady, rhythmic hum, a reassuring constant that blended with the exotic symphony of birds, insects, and the rustle of unseen creatures in the underbrush.

We were not far from the dock when a sudden crash shattered our focus. Branches snapped, and before us, Anton and his henchmen emerged like specters from the undergrowth, armed and with a dangerous glint in their eyes. Their ambush was perfectly timed; we had become complacent in our victory.

I could feel Isaac's tension from where he sat beside me, his body rigid. He glanced at his bandaged arm, then at the men blocking our path, his face paling. It was as if his injury served as a physical manifestation of our vulnerability.

"Keep calm," Dr. Bellamy murmured, her hands tightening on the wheel.

Anton stepped forward, his smile cold and unwelcoming. "You've been quite elusive," he called out to us, his voice carrying an edge that sliced through the humid air.

Isaac shifted uncomfortably, swallowing hard. "We can't let them take it," he whispered fiercely.

Dr. Bellamy nodded silently, her gaze calculating as she assessed our options. There was no easy way out; we were cornered on a narrow path with treacherous wilderness on either side and menace ahead.

Isaac's breathing quickened, each inhale shallow and laboured. I reached over to squeeze his shoulder in silent support, but he barely seemed to notice. His eyes were fixed on Anton's group as they started to fan out, enclosing us.

"It's okay," I reassured him, though my own heart raced with fear. "We've faced worse."

But had we? This was not like solving puzzles or navigating ancient ruins; this was real danger—the kind that could end with us losing everything we had fought for.

Isaac leaned back against the seat, closing his eyes for a moment as if gathering himself. When he opened them again, there was a flicker of determination there despite the panic that lurked beneath.

"We need a plan," he said through gritted teeth.

Dr. Bellamy glanced at him, nodding once more before shifting her attention back to Anton and his men who were now ominously quiet—a stillness before the storm.

I felt Isaac's panic as my own—a shared tremor between allies who had come too far to give up now. His injury might have limited him physically, but I knew his mind was racing for a solution just as desperately as mine.

———— ∘ ◦ ◉ ◦ ∘ ————

Anton and his intimidating crew loom above us, their ominous presence forming a trap, a cage of danger from which escape seems impossible. Amidst this imminent threat, Dr. Bellamy's gaze finds mine. Within that fleeting, nearly imperceptible exchange, I perceive her calculation, her brilliant mind rapidly evaluating our precarious situation. She's assessing our odds, minutely examining our thin sliver of hope against the overwhelming force that is Anton's formidable strength.

"Rebecca," she says, her voice steady but with an undercurrent of urgency, "we need to think this through. There's no shame in compliance if it keeps us safe. The Amulet isn't worth our lives."

I nod, knowing she's right but feeling the weight of betrayal settle in my chest. The Amulet pieces in my bag suddenly feel like they're burning a hole through the fabric.

Anton strides forward, his boots kicking up gravel with each step, his smile as sharp as the blade I'm sure he has hidden somewhere on him. His men fan out behind him, a silent and threatening backdrop to the main act.

"Hand them over, Rebecca," Anton calls out, his voice dripping with triumph before I've even moved. "Each piece of your precious Austral Amulet."

My fingers tremble as I reach into my bag and touch the cool metal of the Amulet pieces. They're intricately crafted, each one a chapter of history and a fragment of my family's legacy. I can almost hear Great-Gran Eleanor's voice whispering stories of adventure and urging me to be brave.

With painstaking slowness, I extract the pieces from my bag, laying them with deliberate care into Anton's eagerly awaiting palm. He scrutinizes each fragment with a discerning gaze, as though he's appraising rare jewels, his smug satisfaction resonating in the quiet huffs of air he exhales.

"Bravo," he utters, his voice thick with feigned commendation as he secures each piece snugly within the depths of his coat pocket. "With this simple gesture, you've effectively sealed my triumph."

The words sear into me, a biting reminder of the power shift, yet I cling determinedly to Dr. Bellamy's sage counsel, her words serving as an anchor: the wellbeing of ourselves eclipses the significance of this fleeting clash.

⸻ • ● • ⸻

The air grew heavy with the scent of defeat as Anton's smug expression cut deeper than any physical wound could. The lush foliage of the island seemed to recoil in silence, as if nature itself was bracing for the fallout of his victory. I watched him handle the pieces of the Austral Amulet with a mix of reverence and greed, the kind that only a man blinded by ambition could muster.

"You don't understand what you're doing," I said, my voice steady despite the tremors of fear that threatened to betray me. "That Amulet... it's not just some trinket you can claim. There's a curse on it—a curse that will latch onto you and your bloodline if you take it for selfish reasons."

Anton chuckled, his eyes never leaving the glittering prize in his hands. "Curses," he scoffed. "Superstitions of the feeble-minded who fear their own shadows. I am a man of action, Rebecca. A man who shapes his own destiny."

I clenched my fists, frustration boiling within me. It wasn't just about losing the Amulet; it was about all we had gone through—the struggles, the revelations, and the bonds we forged along this perilous journey. And here stood Anton, ready to unravel it all with his arrogance.

247

"You're making a mistake," I pressed on, unable to let his ignorance go unchallenged. "This isn't a game or some adventure story where you get to be the hero at the end. The curse is real, and it will consume you just as it has threatened to consume my family for generations."

Dr. Bellamy stood beside me, her expression grim but resolute. Even Isaac, with his arm hanging limply at his side, emanated defiance in the face of Anton's smugness.

But Anton merely waved a dismissive hand in my direction as if swatting away an insignificant fly. "Let it come then," he said with a dangerous glint in his eye. "I have faced challenges greater than old wives' tales and emerged victorious every time."

I knew then that there was no piercing the armour of his hubris—no warning that could sway him from the path he was so determined to tread. He believed himself untouchable, above the ancient forces that had driven men like my great-great-grandfather Jeremiah to madness and despair.

And as Anton turned away from us with our legacy in his grasp, I couldn't help but wonder if he truly understood the gravity of what he had just set into motion—or if he cared at all.

Dr. Bellamy stepped forward, her voice steady as the leaves rustling in the wind. "Anton, heed the warning," she said. "History is replete with tales of those who trifled with sacred relics to their own ruin."

I watched Anton's face as Dr. Bellamy spoke, his features hard like the craggy cliffs we had scaled to retrieve the amulet pieces. His men shifted uneasily behind him, their weapons a stark contrast to the scholarly resolve in Dr. Bellamy's eyes.

She continued, unfazed by the barrels aimed at us. "The ancient Egyptians believed in Ma'at, harmony and balance. They cursed their tombs not out of malice but to protect that balance from being disturbed by greed." Her gaze never wavered from Anton's. "And when that balance was disrupted, there were consequences—not just for the thief but for all they held dear."

I could see Anton's grip tighten around the amulet, his knuckles whitening. Dr. Bellamy's words seemed to conjure images of sandstorms erasing grandiose empires and locusts devouring crops.

"There are accounts," she pressed on, "of conquerors who took what was not theirs to take, whose names have been lost to history along with their bloodlines. They vanished not because they were forgotten but because they ceased to exist."

Anton laughed, a hollow sound that did not reach his eyes. "Fairy tales to scare children," he scoffed.

But Dr. Bellamy did not relent. "Consider the Koh-i-Noor diamond, said to bring misfortune to any man who wears it." She paused for effect, and even I felt a shiver run down my spine despite the tropical heat clinging to my skin. "It has passed through dynasties, and with each transfer came bloodshed and betrayal."

A bead of sweat trailed down Anton's temple as he listened, though whether it was from the humidity or a creeping dread, I couldn't tell.

"The Hope Diamond is another," Dr. Bellamy went on relentlessly. "Its owners suffered madness, suicides, financial ruin... All documented, all very real." She took a step closer to Anton and his men backed away slightly as if her words were a physical force pushing them back.

"Anton Kozlov," she addressed him directly now, her voice dropping to a grave whisper that somehow carried more weight than if she had shouted. "You stand at a precipice with history as your witness."

Anton's once cocksure smirk flickered like a dying flame in a storm.

"Do you truly believe you are immune?" she asked pointedly. "That you can harness the power of something so steeped in tradition and legend without consequence?"

For a moment—just one—I saw it: The crack in Anton's armor of arrogance. The glint of doubt in his eyes as he considered not just his fate but that of his descendants.

Dr. Bellamy wasn't just recounting history; she was painting a future—a bleak one where Anton's lineage wilted under the weight of his choices today.

"The curse does not care for bravado or disbelief," Dr. Bellamy finished.

The air around us grew heavy with thought—the unspoken acknowledgement that some things in this world remained beyond our understanding and control.

I looked at Anton then and saw something new in his demeanour: fear. Fear that perhaps we were not just spouting legends but truths that resonated through time—a fear that perhaps he had indeed gone too far this time.

In an instant, it caught my eye—a subtle flicker, a hint of doubt that danced behind his eyes, betraying his confident facade.

"You fail to grasp the significance of what's in your hands," I declared, my voice steady and even, belying the tumultuous emotions swirling within me. "This is not simply an object for hoarding away in some dark corner. Its true purpose is far more profound—it is a catalyst for unity, a means to forge bonds of camaraderie as we navigate the trials and triumphs of our shared existence."

Anton sneered at me, but I could tell my words had taken root. "Unity?" he scoffed. "What do you know about unity? You're just a kid."

I looked him straight in the eye, my resolve hardening. "More than you might think," I countered. "This journey—it wasn't just about finding pieces of an old relic. It was about facing fears, overcoming challenges... together. That's where its true power lies."

Dr. Bellamy stepped forward then, her voice echoing my sentiment with the weight of her vast knowledge. "Rebecca is right," she said. "History is replete with tales of those who sought power through objects like these. It never ends well—especially when those objects are bound by curses intended to protect them."

Anton's crew stirred restlessly once more, their eyes flickering back and forth from their leader to our group. They, too, felt the change in the atmosphere.

Anton looked down at the Amulet in his hands, and for a moment he seemed smaller, less sure of himself. The harsh lines of greed softened into something resembling fear—a realization that perhaps he was meddling with forces beyond his control.

"I've seen men like you before," Dr. Bellamy continued, her tone insistent but not unkind. "They become consumed by their conquests, blind to the consequences until it's too late."

A tense silence fell over us like a shroud. I could hear nothing but our breathing and the distant call of a bird—a stark contrast to the gravity of our standoff.

Finally, Anton spoke again, his voice low and grudgingly thoughtful. "And what would happen if this curse came upon me? Upon my family?"

"The curse is very specific," Dr. Bellamy replied solemnly. "It targets those who would use the Amulet for selfish gain, who disregard its purpose to bind rather than divide."

I observed Anton intently as he absorbed her words, his expression inscrutable as he meticulously weighed each syllable against an invisible scale known only to him.

"It's not worth it," I added. "Not for gold or glory or whatever else you're seeking. The cost is too high."

For a long moment, nobody moved.

Then slowly, reluctantly, Anton extended his arm back toward me—the Amulet resting on his open palm.

"Take it," he said gruffly. "But if this is some trick..."

"It's no trick," Dr. Bellamy assured him gently.

I reached out and carefully took the Amulet back into my custody.

"Remember this moment," I told Anton as I wrapped my fingers around it protectively. "Remember that sometimes walking away is the bravest thing you can do."

He gave a barely noticeable nod and then signalled his troops to depart.

While they withdrew to their conveyances, Anton, with his head lowered, gradually began to walk away.

⸻ · ◦ ◉ ◦ · ⸻

With the Amulet back in my trembling hands, I could feel its warmth seeping into my skin, a silent hum of ancient energy pulsating against my palm. I lifted my gaze to Anton, who stood a few paces away, his posture deflated, the lines of his face softened by the dawning realization of what he'd nearly unleashed upon himself and his kin.

"Anton," I began, my voice steady despite the adrenaline still coursing through me. "I understand your desire for power, for control, but in the raw truth of this moment, my heart chooses forgiveness as the path to healing, for both of us, and to honour the journey that has led us here."

He stared at me, a flicker of confusion crossing his features before they settled into an expression I couldn't quite decipher—was it relief? Gratitude? I couldn't be sure.

The Austral Amulet in my grasp began to thrum more insistently, as if it resonated with the words of forgiveness and understanding I'd extended towards Anton. And then, before our astonished eyes, it started to transform. The five separate pieces we'd tirelessly sought and safeguarded began to glow with a warm light that grew brighter until we had to shield our eyes.

When the light dimmed and we dared to look again, the Amulet had changed—it was no longer segmented but had melded into a single golden form that radiated a gentle heat and a soft golden light. The intricate patterns on its surface seemed to dance and shift, telling the story of our journey—the trials faced, the unity forged between Isaac, Dr. Bellamy, and me.

We all drew back in awe at witnessing this sight. Even Anton took an involuntary step backwards, his eyes wide with wonder and something akin to reverence. The transformation of the Austral Amulet was a testament not just to the power of unity but also to the resolution of my quest—a quest that had begun with whispers of adventure from my great-grandmother Eleanor and led me here to this pivotal moment.

The air around us was charged with a sense of completion and peace as if the Amulet itself exhaled a sigh of contentment at being made whole once more.

Chapter 19

The weight of the Amulet in my hand was nothing compared to the weight of our experiences. As we stood on the soft sands of the island, a quiet understanding passed between Isaac, Dr. Bellamy, and me. Our eyes met, each pair carrying its own unique blend of relief, fatigue, and pride. We were saying goodbye to more than just a place; we were parting with a chapter of our lives that had changed us irrevocably.

The morning sun stretched long shadows across the beach as we loaded our gear onto the ship. I felt the familiar weight of the Amulet nestled in the fabric of my pocket, its smooth surface a tangible reminder of the journey we had undertaken together. With one last glance at the lush greenery that had tested our resolve and forged unbreakable bonds, I stepped onto the deck, embracing the reassuring solidity of the sturdy wood beneath my feet.

Isaac was quieter than usual, his arm in a sling but his spirit unbroken. His eyes lingered on the island's silhouette, and I knew he was replaying every challenge we'd faced: from scaling treacherous mountains to navigating ancient ruins. He had confronted his deepest fears head-on and emerged stronger for it.

Dr. Bellamy stood at the railing, her gaze lost in the horizon. She was always the one with answers, our guiding star through history's murky waters. But now, she seemed contemplative, as if she was reassessing every historical fact she'd ever known in light of our incredible journey.

Leaning against the ship's cool metal railings, I savored each deep breath as if it were my first in ages. The salty tang of the sea air invigorated me, infusing my lungs with a newfound sense of freedom. In the palm of my hand, I clutched the pendant Eleanor had entrusted to me all those years ago—a simple keepsake that had evolved into something far more profound, a talisman of courage and guidance that had guided me through the darkest of times.

As the ship slowly pulled away from the shore, a heavy silence enveloped us, rendering words unnecessary in the face of our shared emotions. With each gentle wave that lapped against the hull, it seemed to carry away echoes of our trials and triumphs on that distant island—the very crucible where legends were born and where our own story was irrevocably etched into the annals of time.

During those first few hours at sea, my mind wandered back through every moment since reading Eleanor's will. I thought about how I'd felt invisible in my life before this adventure—unsure and insignificant—and how Eleanor had seen something in me that I hadn't been able to see in myself.

With every mile that widened between us and the island, I felt my old insecurities slip further away into the ocean's depths. The girl who had nervously opened Eleanor's diary in her attic hideaway seemed like a stranger now. That girl could never have imagined she would be here today, returning home with an artifact of immeasurable power and history safely in her care.

Isaac eventually broke away from his introspective trance and approached me with a hesitant smile. "You know," he began, "when we were kids playing adventurers in your backyard... I never dreamed we'd end up living out a real one."

I chuckled at that—a sound surprisingly free from worry or weariness—and met his eyes with newfound confidence. "Me neither," I admitted. "But here we are."

Dr. Bellamy joined us then, her hands wrapped around a steaming mug of tea from below deck. She handed one to Isaac and then to me before claiming a spot by my side.

"I've spent years uncovering histories behind glass cases," she said thoughtfully. "But this..." She gestured to all of us with her mug before continuing. "This was history coming alive—history we were part of shaping."

The sun began its slow descent toward evening as we sailed on silent waters—each sunset hue reflecting on our faces as if to paint us anew.

We had faced dangers together; dangers that could have torn us apart or worse—ended us—but instead had forged an unbreakable bond among us all.

In those quiet hours aboard the ship heading home, it became clear how much each one of us had transformed:

Isaac had walked through his anxieties like passing shadows under noonday suns; he no longer allowed fear to dictate his actions but rather accepted it as part of who he was—a piece that made him whole.

Dr. Bellamy found exhilaration outside academic halls—a thirst for adventure awakened within her scholarly heart. Her knowledge wasn't just theoretical anymore; it was lived, breathed—a part of her story now too.

And me? I found strength within myself that Eleanor always knew existed; strength not only to lead but also to trust—in others and myself.

The Amulet hummed with energy against my chest—a reminder not just of what we found but also what we sought within ourselves: courage, friendship... unity.

As night cloaked us under its starlit mantle, we continued our silent voyage homeward—the ocean's vastness a fitting parallel for our own internal landscapes expanded by this extraordinary adventure—an adventure none of us would ever forget.

⁕ ⚬ ◉ ◐ ⚬ ⁕

As our car's tyre grated against the pebbly path, the familiar sound resonated with an air of anticipation. Willow Creek's boundary loomed ahead, marking the threshold of familiarity and the promise of home. Yet, the concept of "home" felt distant, almost surreal, after the trials we had endured. Despite the flood of memories threatening to overwhelm us, there was no room for nostalgia. Isaac, Dr. Bellamy, and I remained steadfast in our determination, focused on the singular mission that lay ahead.

We turned onto an overgrown path that led to the family's ancestral land—a swath of untouched forest rumored to have been in my family since Jeremiah's time. I could feel the weight of the Austral Amulet in my pocket, its presence both comforting and daunting.

"We're almost there," I murmured, more to myself than to my companions. Isaac nodded, his eyes fixed on the path ahead. Dr. Bellamy consulted Jeremiah's journal one last time, her finger tracing the faded lines of his handwriting.

As we arrived at a clearing encircled by ancient oaks, I felt an inexplicable pull toward its center. The trees stood like silent sentinels guarding a secret long kept from the world. This was where we would break the curse—a place where history mingled with the present, where time itself seemed to pause in reverence.

Dr. Bellamy parked at the edge of the clearing and cut the engine. We stepped out into the hush of nature, each footfall a whisper against the earth. I led them to the center of the clearing, where wildflowers dotted the grass like flecks of paint on a vast green canvas.

"We need to be careful," Dr. Bellamy said as she unloaded our supplies from the back of the SUV. "Whatever we do here today will echo through your family's history."

I nodded, acutely aware of her words' weight as I took out the amulet pieces from my pocket and laid them gently on a bed of moss at my feet.

The late afternoon sun filtered through the leaves, casting dappled shadows that danced across our makeshift altar. We moved around it with deliberate care, placing candles at cardinal points around the clearing and lighting them with matches that flared brightly before settling into a steady glow.

Dr. Bellamy unfurled an old cloth—once vibrant but now muted with age—and spread it beside our circle of candles. "This belonged to your great-grandmother Eleanor," she explained as I helped her smooth out its creases. "It seems fitting that it should be here now."

Isaac was quiet as he gathered kindling for a small fire we'd need later on. His movements were sure and efficient despite his injured arm, which he cradled close to his body when he thought no one was looking.

As we prepared, a swell of gratitude flooded my heart, washing away any lingering doubts or fears. In the presence of these two individuals, who had transcended the roles of mere companions to become cherished friends, I felt an unbreakable bond forged from shared experiences and unwavering support. It was a connection rooted in something deeper than blood or time—a connection that buoyed my spirits and fortified my resolve as we embarked on our journey together.

We stood back for a moment to survey our work: candles flickering like stars come down to earth, Eleanor's cloth lying patiently beside our circle, and above us, branches reaching out as if to embrace us in this sacred act.

"Are you ready?" Isaac asked me, his voice steady but laced with an undercurrent of emotion I knew mirrored my own.

I took a deep breath and nodded once before stepping into our carefully arranged circle. The Austral Amulet lay before me—holding stories untold and hardships overcome.

Closing my eyes, I granted myself a moment of reflection, allowing memories to flood my mind like a torrential river. I recalled Eleanor's enchanting tales, woven from a tapestry of dreams and reality. I remembered the feeling of invisibility that had once shrouded me within my own family, the lack of confidence that had plagued my every step. Yet here I stood, on the precipice of triumph, having embarked on a perilous quest with uncertainty as my only companion.

With Isaac and Dr. Bellamy steadfast at my side, we confronted each challenge head-on, our resolve tested and strengthened with every trial we faced. And through it all, our bonds grew stronger, forged in the fires of adversity, uniting us in a shared purpose that transcended the boundaries of time and space.

My heart swelled with emotions too complex to name as I opened my eyes again and reached for the amulet—looking and study the words on it carefully.

"Let's begin," Dr. Bellamy said.

We recited words written centuries ago by Jeremiah himself—a chant that seemed almost like a song lost in time but found again in this moment of need. Our voices rose together, blending with the rustle of leaves and crackle of flames from our small fire.

The world around us hushed even further as if nature itself was holding its breath while we performed this ancient rite—each word spoken with respect and care for what was about to unfold within this hallowed ground.

The sky stretched above us like an ancient canvas, painted with hues of twilight that seemed to hold their breath. I stood there, the golden Amulet heavy in my hands, not just with its physical weight but with the legacy it carried. This was it—the moment that my great-great-grandfather Jeremiah had sought, the moment my great-grandmother Eleanor had prepared me for in stories veiled as mere fairy tales. I felt their presence in the stillness, the countless generations watching from a place beyond time.

My friends, Isaac and Dr. Bellamy, stood by me, their faces etched with solemnity and awe. We had become a family of sorts, bound not by blood but by shared trials and unwavering loyalty. Isaac, with his arm bandaged and sling-bound, offered a nod of encouragement, his eyes reflecting the fading light. Dr. Bellamy's gaze was fixed on the Amulet, her scholarly poise giving way to a reverence reserved for artifacts of true power.

I swallowed hard, the air crisp as it filled my lungs. My voice began as a whisper, steadying as I recited the prayer engraved upon the Amulet's surface—a prayer I hadn't known I remembered until this very moment:

"Lord of ages past and days to come,
In Your hands we place our line.
With this plea, let Your will be done:
Break these chains that bind."

The words were more than a plea; they were an invocation that echoed a scripture about liberation—a cry for freedom that had resonated through time:

"To proclaim liberty to captives,
And freedom to those who are oppressed,

To break every yoke that enslaves,
And bless those long distressed."

As the last word of the prayer is spoken, a sudden illumination—a bright, pulsating light—bursts from the Amulet, bathing everyone in a warm glow. It's as if the very air around us hums with an ancient tune, vibrating with the resonance of countless generations. The light envelops us like a cocoon spun from threads of sunbeams. It's impossible to look away or even to blink; it's as if the light itself commands our full attention.

My heart pounds in my chest, not with fear but with a powerful surge of something akin to relief. It's as if the very burden of history—the weight that has long pressed upon my family—begins to lift and dissipate like mist under the morning sun. I can feel Isaac's hand grip mine tighter, his breath held in awe or perhaps in a silent prayer of his own. Dr. Bellamy stands close by, her eyes wide with scholarly fascination that this moment—this incredible, impossible moment—is real.

The Amulet itself feels alive in my hands, its surface warmer than before but not uncomfortably so. It thrums as if it holds a heartbeat, and I can't help but wonder if it's rejoicing in its own way. I think of Eleanor and Jeremiah and all those who came before me, and I can almost sense their presence here with us, their whispers carried on the wings of the light.

And then, as gently as it began, the supernatural light starts to fade. It recedes slowly, drawing back into the Amulet like the tide pulling away from the shore. The golden form dims but continues to shine with an inner luster that seems to promise that its power remains intact—only now it's power for good.

As the last vestiges of light disappear completely, leaving us under the same starry sky we've known all our lives, a profound silence follows. No one dares to speak; no one moves. There's only the soft rustle of leaves in the gentle night breeze and our own quiet breaths.

A sensation of peace settles over us, wrapping around our shoulders like a blanket woven from tranquility itself. The curse has been lifted; I can feel it in my bones, an unshakable certainty that speaks louder than any words could. We stand together in that silence for what feels like an eternity but must only be minutes.

I release a breath I didn't realize I was holding and look over at Isaac. His eyes meet mine, and there's an understanding there—a shared experience that has changed us both forever. Dr. Bellamy steps forward slightly, her gaze lingering on where the Amulet now rests against my chest.

"We did it," she says, her voice imbued with wonder and respect for what we've just witnessed.

"We did," I echo back just as quietly.

The curse is lifted—the truth of that statement fills me with an elation that is almost too much to bear. But more than anything else, I feel gratitude: for Eleanor's faith in me; for Isaac and Dr. Bellamy's unwavering support; for Anton's change of heart; for every twist and turn on this long road that led us here.

In this moment of tranquillity, everything else falls away—the fear of being pursued by Anton or his men; the treacherous paths we've travelled; even the pain and doubt that have dogged our steps along this journey—and all that remains is peace.

The peace within us reflects outward into the world around us—the land of Willow Creek seems to breathe easier tonight—and within my heart I know: we've not only broken a curse but also forged something new—something good—in its place.

⸻ · ◦ ◉ ◦ · ⸻

I stood there, my feet rooted to the earth of my ancestors, the golden glow of the Austral Amulet fading from my palms. My heart was still racing from the prayer, a sacred plea to break chains not seen but heavily borne. The night air wrapped around us like a velvet shawl as Isaac, Dr. Bellamy, and I clung to each other in a group embrace, our breaths mingling in the charged silence that followed the light show of liberation.

Isaac's grip on my shoulder tightened, and I felt his chest rise against mine as he drew in a deep breath. "Rebecca," he started, his voice carrying a tremor of emotion I'd never heard from him before. "You... we... did it." He stepped back just enough to look at me, his eyes reflecting starlight and something deeper – respect, perhaps, or maybe realization. "I mean, you did it. You faced down Anton with nothing but words and conviction. You brought us here, led us through everything." His uninjured arm swept out toward the expanse of our surroundings. "This... it's all because of you."

Dr. Bellamy stepped out of our embrace but kept one hand on each of our shoulders. "Indeed," she agreed with a nod that held decades of scholarly weight behind it. "Rebecca, your bravery has been the beacon on this journey. The strength you've shown, not just in facing physical challenges but also in confronting your own doubts and fears..." She paused, her eyes gleaming with what could only be pride.

"Your resolve has been unwavering," she continued. "And the unity you fostered among us – it was more than just a means to an end; it was the very essence that allowed us to succeed."

The cool breeze seemed to carry their words away into the night as I looked between them, absorbing their gratitude and admiration. Isaac's injury hadn't slowed him down; instead, it had brought out a courage I knew he always had within him. And Dr. Bellamy's vast knowledge had guided us when we were lost in more ways than one.

It wasn't just my journey; it was ours – every puzzle solved, every trial faced, we did together.

"Thank you," I whispered at first, then repeated louder with newfound strength in my voice. "Thank you both for believing in me... for standing by me when things got tough."

Isaac shook his head slightly as if to dismiss my thanks and said earnestly, "No, Rebecca. Thank you. For not giving up on me when I almost did." His voice broke slightly with vulnerability that mirrored the day he told us about his panic attacks – a revelation that had bound us even closer.

Dr. Bellamy's smile was soft around the edges but fierce at its core. "In all my years," she mused aloud, "I have seldom seen such a profound transformation catalyzed by ancient relics." Her gaze flicked to where the Amulet lay tranquil in my hand.

"I've read about it in dusty old texts," she said softly, almost reverently. "But witnessing your growth – our growth – it's something entirely different."

Isaac's laughter then was a melody woven with relief and delight. "Imagine," he marveled, shaking his head in disbelief, "once viewing adventures merely as diversions from the ennui of home." His gaze shifted to Dr. Bellamy before returning to mine with a sincere look. "This quest... It didn't serve as a retreat; it was about confronting everything directly."

"Salvation played a role in my journey as well," Isaac went on. The disappearance of my father made the prospect of such a quest daunting. Yet now I see, just as he realized, that victory is attainable. How I yearn for him to behold this scene.

Rebecca and Dr. Bellamy offered Isaac smiles filled with encouragement and fondness.

"We're also facing the deepest parts of who we are," Dr. Bellamy added with a reflective tone.

I gave a confirming nod because she was correct; our battle was as much with our own inner struggles as it was with any tangible threats or shrewd foes.

"The love and unity," I murmured aloud what we were all thinking.

"It's what Eleanor always talked about," Isaac said quietly.

"And what Jeremiah knew would save us all along," Dr. Bellamy finished for him.

I held up the Amulet once more, watching how ordinary it looked now compared to minutes ago when its power had surged through every fiber of my being – our beings – breaking curses laid by fear and hatred centuries ago.

We stood together under the stars that seemed to approve of our small circle of warmth in the cold night air. We had done more than find pieces of an ancient artifact; we had pieced together fragments of ourselves that we hadn't even known were missing.

We stayed like that for some time – not speaking much but saying everything that needed to be said in silence filled with mutual respect and understanding forged through fire and trials none of us would ever forget.

And as I finally lowered the Amulet from its silent testimony against the night sky, I felt not just its weight but also its promise: unity could indeed turn curses into blessings and fears into victories.

It was a lesson engraved upon my heart now – one that Eleanor had known all along and one that Isaac and Dr. Bellamy helped me live out loud: Love and unity aren't just lofty ideals; they're powerful forces when wielded by brave souls willing to walk through darkness together until dawn breaks anew.

Chapter 20

The familiar creak of the front gate, the scent of jasmine from mom's garden—it was all the same, yet I stood at the threshold, a stranger to my own home. My hand trembled as I lifted it to knock. The door swung open before my knuckles could rap against the wood, and there stood my parents, their faces etched with worry lines like ancient scripts detailing days of distress.

"Rebecca!" Mom's voice cracked as she threw her arms around me, her embrace engulfing me in warmth and the faint scent of vanilla from her apron. Dad followed, his strong arms wrapping around us both, a protective shield as always. I could feel their hearts pounding against mine, their relief flooding through me like a balm.

They pulled back to look at me, really look at me, and I saw something shift in their eyes. Perhaps it was the way I held myself now—shoulders back, eyes no longer darting away but meeting theirs squarely—or maybe it was the calm that had settled over me like a cloak. Whatever it was, they saw it.

"Bec, you've grown," Dad said softly, his voice tinged with a mixture of awe and something else—respect? "Not just in height." He chuckled weakly but there was truth in his jest.

Mom cupped my face in her hands. "We were so worried," she whispered. "But look at you... You have this... serenity about you."

I could only nod, words lodged behind a lump in my throat. How could I begin to tell them of the trials faced, the fears conquered? It would come out in time; for now, I basked in their acceptance of this new version of me.

A ruckus broke our reunion; my brothers barrelled down the stairs with all the grace of a landslide. "Becca's back! Do we still get to eat her share of dessert?" Zack joked as he tousled my hair. Josh elbowed him aside to get a better look at me.

"Cut it out," Josh said to Zack before turning his attention back to me. His eyes narrowed slightly as he studied my face. "You're different," he observed quietly.

Zack rolled his eyes but then paused mid-mockery, actually taking a moment to regard me seriously. "Yeah...

you're like one of those heroes in your books," he conceded with a smirk that softened into something akin to admiration.

We gathered in the living room—my old sanctuary—where they pelted me with questions that danced around the edges of what had transpired: How was Dr. Bellamy? Was Isaac okay? Did we really find what we were looking for?

With each answer I gave, more than just recounting events unfolded; I shared glimpses of a journey that had reshaped my very soul. And as they listened—a real attentive listen—I saw respect bloom where once there had been dismissiveness.

The teasing dwindled as our conversation deepened into the evening. We spoke of fear and courage; loss and discovery; but most importantly, unity—a theme that had stitched itself into every aspect of my adventure.

"You've changed more than we thought," Tim said after a stretch of silence that followed my recounting of how we'd found unity in our darkest hour on the mountain descent.

Josh nodded solemnly beside him. "We always thought you were off in your own world with those books and daydreams," he admitted. "But turns out you were preparing for something bigger than any of us could've imagined."

There it was—an acknowledgment that moved beyond words—a bridge between worlds I never thought would meet: theirs and mine.

In the embrace of family unity—a tapestry woven from threads of chaos and understanding—I experienced a profound emotional fullness, unlike any other sensation I had ever known. Home transcended the confines of mere bricks and mortar; it became this moment, this gathering of hearts and minds that finally saw each other with clarity and empathy.

And as night crept upon us with our shared laughter echoing off the walls, I realized this adventure hadn't just led me to uncover secrets buried by time or face down an age-old curse—it had guided me home to find what I'd longed for all along: belonging.

Walking through the familiar halls of Willow Creek High, I felt the eyes on me. I was the same Rebecca who left, yet entirely different. Gone was the girl who would shrink at the back of the classroom, her voice seldom rising above a whisper. In her place stood someone new—someone forged by trials and adventures, by unity and ancient curses now broken.

I weaved through clusters of my peers with a stride that felt both strange and exhilarating. Where hesitation once anchored my steps, purpose now propelled them. The pendant around my neck, no longer glowing with secrets or history, was a simple adornment to the outside world. To me, it was a medal of honour, a symbol of the journey and the lessons learned.

"Rebecca!" called out Mrs. Donnelly as I passed her room. The history teacher's voice used to make me flinch—expecting to be called out for daydreaming about far-off places during her lectures. Not today.

Pausing at her door, I offered a smile that felt as natural as my own skin. "Good morning, Mrs. Donnelly," I greeted warmly.

She returned the smile with a gleam in her eye that acknowledged our unspoken understanding. "I've been hearing stories about your travels. Would you consider sharing them with the class someday?"

The invitation caught me off guard, but to my own surprise, I found myself eagerly accepting. "I'd love to," I responded without hesitation, feeling an unexpected thrill at the thought of standing before my classmates.

In class, when discussions veered toward topics of history or geography—subjects once content to swirl around my daydreams—I found myself participating with enthusiasm that resonated from within. No longer content to let others shape the narrative, I wove in perspectives gleaned from experiences beyond these walls.

"You bring up an excellent point about cultural exchange," Mr. Jacobs nodded approvingly during social studies as I argued for the tangible benefits of understanding foreign customs—a lesson learned firsthand.

The bell rang for lunch, signalling a temporary retreat from academia, but not from the shift in dynamics that continued to ripple around me.

In the cafeteria, I chose a table where once I would have sat in silence, but now I initiated conversations. I spoke of local customs from distant lands with vivid details that painted pictures more colourful than any textbook illustration.

"Wow, Rebecca," marvelled Lucas from across the table as he hung on every word about an island festival I described. "It's like you're a different person."

A chuckle escaped me before I could temper it with modesty. "Maybe not different," I corrected him gently, "just more myself than ever before."

⸺ ● ◉ ◉ ● ⸺

The dust of the quest had settled, and the once treacherous paths they traversed had become mere memories, etched into the backdrops of their minds. The camaraderie of the trio—Rebecca, Isaac, and Dr. Bellamy—had grown into a silent understanding, a shared narrative of overcoming and triumph.

Isaac stood at the threshold of his home, gazing at the horizon stretching beyond Wollow Creek. The adventure had ignited something within him, a flame that no mundane routine could extinguish. He clutched an envelope—a beacon of his newfound resolve—bearing the insignia of a prestigious international volunteer program. It was his leap towards a future unbound by fear, a testament to his growth.

His fingers brushed against the paper, tracing the raised seal as if to confirm its reality. Once, his past self would have recoiled from such an opportunity, allowing the tendrils of panic to dictate his choices. But those days now felt like distant echoes from another life. With each step taken on their journey for the Austral Amulet, with each obstacle surmounted, Isaac had reconstructed himself from the ground up, emerging stronger and more resilient than ever before.

The application had been filled with trepidation; his pen had hovered over the paper more times than he cared to admit. But as he sealed his acceptance, he felt a surge of courage—a departure from the boy who once looked upon change as an insurmountable mountain.

Isaac found himself at the local post office, where community notice boards bore flyers of town events and lost pets. He approached the counter with purposeful strides, handing over his future encapsulated in an envelope to the postal worker. "This goes out today," he said with more confidence than he felt.

As he exited into the bright light of day, Isaac paused for a moment to let it sink in. He was leaving Wollow

Creek—not forever, but long enough to taste a life beyond its familiar borders.

He made his way to Rebecca's house, where she was planting new flowers in her family's garden—another form of growth and renewal. She looked up at his approach, wiping dirt off her hands onto her apron.

"I did it," Isaac announced before she could utter a greeting.

Rebecca stood up straighter, a knowing smile tugging at her lips. "You're going."

He nodded. "I'm going." His voice carried a mixture of excitement and underlying nerves.

"Where to?" Rebecca asked as she leaned on her spade.

"Africa," Isaac replied. "Building schools, helping communities... It's not searching for mystical amulets, but it's something real—something I can do."

Rebecca walked over and hugged him tightly. "I'm proud of you."

As Isaac watched Rebecca's beaming smile and felt the warmth of her hand in his, a swell of emotion surged within him. It wasn't merely pride in her accomplishments; it was a deep-rooted sense of satisfaction that blossomed from his own contributions—a feeling he hadn't truly experienced until this moment.

The days leading up to his departure blurred into a flurry of preparations and farewells that tugged at Isaac's heartstrings with bittersweet pangs. His mother fussed over packing lists while his father offered quiet words of encouragement that bolstered Isaac's resolve.

And then came the day of departure—an early morning with mist still clinging to the edges of Wollow Creek like a soft blanket being pulled away by dawn's light.

Isaac stood beside an old suitcase that had seen better days—the same one that accompanied him on their amulet quest—packed now with essentials for a different kind of adventure.

Dr. Bellamy arrived first to see him off—a gesture that spoke volumes without needing words. She handed him a small leather-bound journal similar to Jeremiah's but empty and waiting for new stories to fill its pages.

"Make your own history," she said with an encouraging smile that warmed Isaac from within.

His family gathered around him; their eyes shone with pride mixed with concern—a cocktail of emotions parents brewed when their children took bold steps into the unknown.

And then there was Rebecca—the steadfast friend who had been by his side through thick and thin—who stood apart from everyone else as if giving him space to breathe in this moment fully.

Isaac hugged each family member in turn before turning to Rebecca last. They shared no tearful goodbyes or dramatic promises; their journey together had already spoken all that needed saying.

"I'll see you soon," Isaac said simply as he shouldered his bag and headed towards Dr. Bellamy's car which would take him to where new adventures awaited—the airport calling him forth into a world larger than Wollow Creek could ever contain.

Rebecca watched in silence as the car dwindled into the distance, gradually merging into the landscape until it became just another fleeting image on the horizon—a vanishing point beyond which lay Isaac's future. Despite the bittersweet ache of parting, she couldn't help but feel a swell of hope within her. Isaac had embraced courage with unwavering resolve, and now he stood poised and ready to greet whatever chapters life intended to inscribe next upon his journey.

———— • ● • • ————

Dr. Bellamy stood amidst the ancient artifacts and timeworn relics of the museum, her eyes alight with a fervor that had been absent before her grand adventure. Her colleagues noted the change in her; the once weary historian now moved with a purposeful grace, her gestures animated as she described her vision for the new exhibit. It was to be a showcase unlike any other the museum had hosted—a narrative woven through time and space, inspired by her recent journey in search of the Austral Amulet.

As she carefully placed an antique compass into a display case, Dr. Bellamy couldn't help but reflect on how the compass's magnetized needle, always seeking north, was akin to her own rejuvenated passion always seeking knowledge. The exhibit would not only feature objects that had guided explorers through history but would also draw parallels to the more personal navigations of the heart and spirit she had witnessed during their quest.

A few weeks later, Dr. Bellamy found herself surrounded by stacks of weathered journals and modern reference books in her office at the museum. The quiet hum of her computer was a stark contrast to the lively crackle of campfires and whispered secrets of ancient ruins that still echoed in her memory. Her fingers danced across the keys with an urgency born from inspiration as she began to draft an academic paper that would share their incredible story intertwined with the Austral Amulet.

She wrote not only as a historian but as someone who had lived the breathing history of the Amulet—its lore, its power, its curse now lifted. With each keystroke, she infused her scholarship with vivid descriptions of hidden chambers and mechanical puzzles, ensuring that readers would not just learn about history—they would feel it pulsate through their veins as she had.

The screen before her filled with words that bridged past and present, merging scholarly research with the adrenaline of discovery. She detailed their challenges and triumphs, never failing to highlight how each piece of the Amulet represented a chapter of unity and understanding—a theme that resonated deeply with her after their shared experiences.

Driven by this deepened connection to history, Dr. Bellamy's eyes sparkled with an infectious enthusiasm. She leaned forward, her voice carrying a rich timbre that captivated her audience. With animated gestures and vivid descriptions, she wove tales of ancient artifacts and the people whose lives they touched. Each story illustrated how relics of the past could resonate with the present, their significance transcending time to shape the world around us.

———— • ◦ ◉ ◦ • ————

The voyage transformed me; back at home, I sensed an alteration in the atmosphere, as if stepping over a boundary into an uncharted phase of my existence. The escapades and challenges had sculpted a persona within me previously unknown. Where I used to observe quietly at the dinner table, I discovered myself engaging eagerly, expressing thoughts that had previously murmured silently in my thoughts.

My parents, initially taken aback by this new assertive daughter, began to lean into it, valuing my input on matters from financial decisions to weekend plans. It was as if they could see the amulet's glow within me, the newfound wisdom it had imparted.

Nick and Zack, my younger brothers, once just boisterous energy and mischief, started to look up to me in a way that tugged at my heartstrings. They were growing up in a world full of noise where it was easy to lose one's self. I saw my reflection in their eyes, remembering how Eleanor's compassion guided me.

"Nick," I said one afternoon as he buzzed around the living room like a bee on an endless search for nectar, "why don't you show me that drawing you've been working on? I bet it's brilliant."

His face lit up as he dashed to his room and returned with a paper crumpled from excitement. It was more than brilliant—it was alive with imagination. "This is amazing," I praised him genuinely. "You have a real talent."

He beamed with pride, something rare for a boy who struggled to find his footing in the still moments.

Zack, on the other hand, often sought attention through pranks and jokes. But beneath that facade was a dreamer who yearned for recognition. "Zack," I started as he planned his next gag, "have you ever thought about using your creativity for storytelling? You could write plays or make films."

His antics paused as he considered this. "Really? You think I could do that?"

"I know you can," I affirmed with a smile.

Josh's quiet demeanor often meant his needs were overlooked in our lively household. But he was no less important. His structured mind and honest views were something I'd come to admire deeply.

"Josh," I said one evening as we all gathered in the living room, "you're really good at putting things in order. Maybe you could help organize some of the family photos or start your own collection."

He looked up from his book, contemplative. "I could categorize them by year... and maybe even event." There was a spark in his eyes—a spark of purpose.

As days turned into weeks, our home began to hum with new energy. My brothers embraced their passions with fervour only matched by their sister's belief in them.

During these moments, I could almost feel Eleanor's presence enveloping me like a comforting embrace. Her spirit lingered in the air, infusing my actions with a gentle guidance that mirrored the encouragement she once bestowed upon me. As I supported and uplifted my brothers, nurturing their dreams and aspirations with the same compassion Eleanor had shown me, her legacy lived on, a testament to the enduring power of love and kinship.

Chapter 21

Sitting at my desk, the late afternoon sun filtered through the window, casting a golden hue over the stack of letters I had yet to open. Most were from distant relatives and friends, eager to hear about the adventures that had kept me away for so long. But one envelope stood out—it was from Isaac. His handwriting was unmistakable, even from across the sea.

I slid my finger under the seal and unfolded the letter. His words brought him to life in my room, as if he were sitting across from me, sharing his stories with that lopsided grin of his.

"Dear Rebecca," it began, "I hope this letter finds you as radiant and grounded as you were when we parted ways.

I write to you from a café in Rome, the city is everything you said it would be and more."

I smiled, remembering our long conversations by the campfire about all the places we'd love to visit. It seemed Isaac was ticking them off his list.

"I've been meaning to write sooner," he continued, "but each day brings a new challenge, a new opportunity to assert my independence. You might remember how I used to be—hesitant and often plagued by doubt."

I did remember. How could I forget? Isaac's struggles had been as real and palpable as the weight of the Austral Amulet once was in my hands.

"But you've shown me that bravery isn't the absence of fear—it's facing it head-on. And that's what I've been doing here, Rebecca. Every time panic tries to claw its way in, I think of your courage and how you faced everything with such determination."

My heart swelled with pride for him. The journey we shared had not only transformed me but Isaac too. We had both found pieces of ourselves along that winding path.

"Your bravery gave me strength then, and it continues to do so now," Isaac wrote. "I'm learning to manage my panic better every day. It's not always easy, but I remind myself that fear is just another puzzle to solve, much like those left by Jeremiah."

I laughed softly at that comparison. Our puzzles had been literal mazes and riddles carved into ancient stones, but

Isaac's analogy wasn't far off. Life was full of enigmas, and fear was certainly one of them.

"I've signed up for an Italian language course," he said next. "And guess what? I'm even taking an art history class! Who would have thought? Me? Studying art?"

That sounded just like him—diving into new experiences with a vigor that was contagious.

"I'm finding bits of myself in places I never thought to look," he concluded before signing off with warm regards and a promise to write again soon.

I placed his letter on my desk and leaned back in my chair. Isaac's journey wasn't just about traveling; it was about discovering himself beyond the confines of Wollow Creek or the shadow of his anxieties. And knowing that he drew inspiration from our shared adventure—that my own transformation had sparked his—made everything we'd been through even more meaningful.

As dusk began to settle outside, another piece of correspondence caught my eye—a scholarly journal bearing Dr. Bellamy's name on the cover. It had arrived earlier in the week but amidst settling back into life at home, I hadn't found a quiet moment to peruse it until now.

Flipping through the pages, I found her article: "The Unity of History: Lessons Learned from the Austral Amulet." The paper detailed our expedition with scholarly precision but also conveyed an undeniable passion for history and adventure—a combination only Dr. Bellamy could master.

She spoke of each Amulet piece not just as relics but as symbols—of courage, unity, growth—and wove our story into the fabric of history itself.

As I read her conclusions about how personal narratives intertwine with historical artifacts to bring them alive in contemporary times, I felt an immense sense of pride welling up inside me. Her paper wasn't just an academic treatise; it was recognition of our journey's significance beyond our small circle—it validated every trial we faced.

Word about her paper spread quickly through academic circles; colleagues began citing her work in their own studies on similar artifacts and expeditions. It laid the groundwork for a new level of respect for Dr. Bellamy among her peers.

She wrote in her acknowledgments: "This paper would not have been possible without Rebecca Harley's unyielding spirit and Isaac Thomason's resourcefulness throughout our unprecedented journey."

I closed the journal with a soft thud, the sound echoing like a final punctuation mark on a story that still pulsed with life within me. Glancing around my room, adorned with mementos from our travels, I couldn't help but feel a sense of gratitude for the memories we had woven together. Each trinket held a tale, each photograph a cherished moment frozen in time—a testament to the transformative journey we had embarked upon, and the indelible mark it had left on my soul.

Dr. Bellamy's career would undoubtedly receive a significant boost thanks to her experiences with us and her firsthand knowledge of the Amulet's powers—powers she helped us understand in depth.

As nightfall draped its velvet cloak over Willow Creek, I reflected on how far we'd all come since those days poring over Jeremiah's journal in Eleanor's attic. Our lives were forever intertwined with history—and with each other—each on a path illuminated by shards of an ancient Amulet and bonds formed under pressure like diamonds deep within the earth's mantle.

Isaac abroad finding his footing amidst Rome's cobblestones; Dr. Bellamy rising through academic ranks armed with knowledge only adventure could teach; and me...well, who knew where my next chapter would lead? But one thing was certain: We were all where we needed to be—for now.

In the soft afternoon light, I stood quietly beside my great-grandmother Eleanor's grave, the Amulet in hand, its surface still warm as if holding the echoes of the sun. The graveyard was a silent place, a garden of stone and memory where whispers of the past rustled through the leaves of old oak trees. The world beyond seemed distant, and for a moment, it was just Eleanor and me, as it had been so many times before.

I crouched down, tracing the etched letters of her headstone with my fingertips—a tactile connection to a woman who had set me on a path of such unexpected adventure. The grass around her grave was lush and green, cared for with a reverence that matched my own.

"Eleanor," I began, my voice barely above a murmur, yet every word carried weight. "I did it." A tear slid down my cheek, but my lips curved into a smile as I recounted the tale. "We found all the pieces of the Amulet—the Austral Amulet. It was nothing like I ever imagined; it was harder, scarier, but also more wondrous."

I glanced down at the golden Amulet resting in my palm. It seemed to vibrate with an ancient power, its energy an affirmation of everything we had been through to bring it back whole. "There were times I thought we wouldn't make it," I confessed. "Times when fear and doubt crept in like shadows at dusk. But then I'd remember something you told me—about courage not being the absence of fear but rather the decision that something else is more important."

The breeze picked up, stirring the leaves and sending a shiver down my spine as if Eleanor were there listening intently to my every word. "You were right about so much," I continued, my voice steadier now. "About unity being our strength. That final piece... it only revealed itself when we all worked together—Isaac with his cleverness despite his fears; Dr. Bellamy with her vast knowledge; even Milo with his... well, let's call it a 'redemption arc.'"

I laughed softly at that last part, knowing Eleanor would have appreciated the humor despite everything.

"And here's something incredible," I said, leaning closer as if sharing a secret between just the two of us. "When we united all five pieces of the Amulet... they fused into this single form." I held up the Amulet for her to see—if spirits could see—and felt an overwhelming sense of pride and accomplishment. "It was like witnessing magic; it was like witnessing hope becoming real."

The silence around us deepened as I fell into reflection on how much had changed—not just in what we achieved but within me. "I found parts of myself I never knew existed," I admitted softly to her memory. "Parts that were brave and strong and... assertive."

The words felt strange on my tongue; they were new friends I was still getting used to.

"I've learned so much about empathy too," I continued, warmth spreading through my chest as I remembered Penelope's words about understanding others' pain and joys as if they were your own. "It's changed how I see people—how I connect with them."

A gust of wind brushed across my face like a caress or perhaps an acknowledgment from Eleanor herself.

"And forgiveness," I added after a moment's pause, remembering Anton's face when he handed back the

Amulet—his features softened by fear and then relief when he realized we bore him no ill will despite his actions against us.

"It's powerful, isn't it? Forgiveness," I mused aloud.

The sun dipped lower in the sky now, painting everything with hues of gold and amber—a celestial backdrop to this intimate conversation.

"I miss you so much," I whispered, allowing myself to feel the full weight of her absence. But there was comfort too in knowing that her spirit lived on—not just in me but in this entire journey and in every life touched by the unity that this Amulet now symbolized.

I rose to my feet slowly, a dichotomy of emotions swirling within me. Anchored by sorrow yet buoyed by the enduring presence of love, I stood poised at the precipice of a new chapter, ready to embrace whatever the future held.

"I promise to keep your legacy alive," I vowed quietly to her gravestone—and to myself. "Through stories and actions and... well, living life as fully as you did."

The tears that fell now were not just from grief but from gratitude too—for having had Eleanor in my life, for being part of this incredible adventure she set me on, for understanding now more than ever what she meant about seizing life with both hands.

"Thank you," I said finally, looking up at the sky that seemed infinite above me—a vast canvas where our stories were written in stars yet unseen. "For everything."

And with those words hanging in the air like a promise made sacred by their sincerity, I turned from Eleanor's grave slowly, clutching the Amulet close—as if holding onto her wisdom one last time before stepping back into a world forever changed by her legacy and now by mine too.

From the Author — Troy C. Wilson

Writing this book was an incredibly personal and emotional journey for me—one that I hold close to my heart. At first glance, Quest for the Austral Amulet might seem like just another young adult adventure novel, full of mystery, hidden secrets, and magical quests. But behind the pages is a deeper, more tender story—one that emerged from my own life, my own heart, and most importantly, my own family.

The main character, Rebecca Harley, is inspired very much by my own daughter. Like many young girls navigating their teenage years, Rebecca struggles to find her place in the world, to feel truly seen and valued, especially in the context of a family with complex needs. My daughter, growing up, had two brothers with special needs who required significant time, care, and emotional energy. And while we loved her dearly, I can look back and see that she often didn't get the time or attention she truly deserved. Writing this book became a way for me to process that—an outlet for reflection, healing, and ultimately, love.

This story was never just about adventure—it became a way of acknowledging my daughter's quiet resilience, her strength, and her longing to be noticed not just as a sibling or a helper, but as her own person. Rebecca's character gave me a voice to say the things I perhaps never said enough: You are seen. You are worthy. You are deeply loved.

There were tears shed in the writing of this book—some of grief, some of gratitude, and many of hope. As a parent, there's no manual for getting everything right. But through storytelling, I was able to explore a relationship I care about deeply and say what needed to be said through the language of fiction. If you're a parent, you may resonate with those moments of realisation—those internal awakenings when you realise how fleeting time can be and how much we wish we could slow down and be more present.

In this way, Quest for the Austral Amulet is more than just an exciting tale—it's a tribute to daughters everywhere who are trying to find their place, and to the parents who are learning, sometimes late, how to love more intentionally. It's a story for families navigating the complexities of life, love, and growth. And above all, it's a reminder that healing can take many forms—including the quiet magic of a well-told story.

As an author, I've written across several genres—from romantic fiction under my pen name Julian T. Westwood, to self-help and emotional well-being books like Calm Cove and It's the Little Things. But this book stands out in a special way. It brought together my passion for storytelling, my love for family, and the quiet ache of missed moments. It reminded me why I write: to reflect, to connect, and to honour the most meaningful parts of our lives.

Enjoyed the Journey?

Your feedback means the world to me!
If you loved this book (or even just liked it), please take a moment to leave a short review on Amazon. It helps other readers discover the story — and it helps me keep writing more!

Simply scan the QR code below to share your thoughts.

Thank you for your support!
— Troy C. Wilson

www.ingramcontent.com/pod-product-compliance
Lightning Source LLC
Chambersburg PA
CBHW030603120726
47904CB00006B/1750